Duffle Bag Cartel 3

Lock Down Publications and Ca$h
Presents
Duffle Bag Cartel 3
A Novel by *Ghost*

Lock Down Publications
P.O. Box 870494
Mesquite, Tx 75187

Visit our website @
www.lockdownpublications.com

Lock Down Publications
Like our page on Facebook: Lock Down Publications @
www.facebook.com/lockdownpublications.ldp
Cover design and layout by: **Dynasty Cover Me**
Book interior design by: **Shawn Walker**
Edited by: **Tammy Jernigan**

Stay Connected with Us!

Text **LOCKDOWN** to 22828 to stay up-to-date with
new releases, sneak peaks, contests and more…
Or **CLICK HERE** to sign up.
Thank you.

Like our page on Facebook:

Lock Down Publications: Facebook

Join Lock Down Publications/The New Era Reading Group

Visit our website @
www.lockdownpublications.com

Follow us on Instagram:

Lock Down Publications: Instagram

Email Us: We want to hear from you!

Submission Guideline.

Submit the first three chapters of your completed manuscript to ldpsubmissions@gmail.com, subject line: Your book's title. The manuscript must be in a .doc file and sent as an attachment. Document should be in Times New Roman, double spaced and in size 12 font. Also, provide your synopsis and full contact information. If sending multiple submissions, they must each be in a separate email.

Have a story but no way to send it electronically? You can still submit to LDP/Ca$h Presents. Send in the first three chapters, written or typed, of your completed manuscript to:

LDP: Submissions Dept
Po Box 870494
Mesquite, Tx 75187

DO NOT send original manuscript. Must be a duplicate.

Provide your synopsis and a cover letter containing your full contact information.

Thanks for considering LDP and Ca$h Presents.

Ghost

Chapter 1

I grabbed Natalia by the neck and slammed her in to the wall. She yelped. "This how you wanna play shit? Huh?"

She started breathing hard. "Ack. Ack. You heard me." Her voice was strained.

I unloosened my grip just enough to let her breathe and kissed her lips. "I'm finna fuck this red pussy. That's what you want, ain't it, bitch?" I was choking her again and yanking her skirt upward. My right hand went into her panties. Her pussy lips were smooth. They appeared freshly shaved. I separated them and slid my middle finger deep into her center. Her labia wrapped around it right away.

She moaned and threw her head back and gagged. I loosened my hold. "That's what you call a Brazilian wax Phoenix. It's nice and smooth for you. I'll always keep this twat up to par for you. I'm yours. Now fuck me into submission." Natalia slapped me and pushed me in the chest.

Before she could get away I grabbed a handful of her hair, and yanked her backward, slung her to the floor and straddled her body. "This what kind of games you wanna play, bitch. Huh?"

"Get off of me, Phoenix! Get off of me right now. I'm not playing." She swung her fists at my face.

That fight made me hard. I ripped her bra from her frame. Her breasts spilled out. I smushed her titties together and sucked hard on first her right nipple and then her left pulling on them until they were rock hard. Two fingers on my right hand worked in and out of her dripping hole. Her thighs were spread wide open.

"Unn. Unn. Unn. Stop. Get the fuck off of me. Get off of me, Phoenix!" Natalia's back arched, her mouth was opened wide.

I covered it with mine. "This is my pussy, Natalia. This my shit. You gon give me the key to the Game. You hear me!" I growled.

The finger fucking continued. Faster and faster. Her lips sucked at the digits. Pussy juice dripped out of her. It saturated her yellow ass cheeks that were humping upward into my hand. Her clit was poking out like the tip of a pinky finger. I could smell the earthly scent of her pussy mixed with her perfume. It was alluring. The scent was enough to encourage me to go harder. The inside of her womb felt like soft, wet velvet. I pulled the fingers out and sucked them into my mouth. The flavor was salty, and pussy rich. I loved it.

"Fuck me, Phoenix. Fuck me hard. Right now. Come on! Please!" Natalia begged.

I was naked in a matter of minutes. Kneeling over her and stroking my piece, while she fingered her pussy and watched me. I crawled closer and placed the head on her lips. She sucked me into her mouth and continued to play with her gap, pinching her clit and running her middle finger in circles around her pearl. Her ass popped up from the ground. Juice leaked from it.

I allowed for her to deep throat me for five minutes. Just when I felt ready to cum, I pulled out, and got between her legs and positioned my dick on her hole. The lips opened right up. I slid through them with one powerful thrust.

"Awwww! Shiiiiit!" She screamed. "Yes!"

Suddenly I was pushing Natalia's knees to her shoulders and fucking her with long strokes as hard as I could. The pussy was so wet that I was slipping in and out rapidly. A squishing sound emanated from her box. My thighs, and balls were drenched. Her scent was so heavy in the air that I became high off it. I was murdering her flower.

"Uhh. Uhh. Uhh. Uhh. Fuck me, Phoenix. Everything. Everything, baby. Everything is yours. Aww. Shit!"

She squeezed her eyes tighter. "Harder. Beat this pussy. Beat this pussy up."

I didn't need her to tell me what to do, I was already doing it. I was killing that shit so bad that I started to hurt myself. My dick plunged deeper and deeper. Our stomachs smacked into one another. I sucked her neck and came hard within the deepest recesses of her cat.

She must've felt it because she began to shake.

"Unnnn. Unnnn. Cum in me. Cum in meeeee Phoenix!" Natalia went into convulsions and dragged her nails across my back.

The door swung open to the hotel room again. Kamya rushed inside with a gun with a silencer in her hand.

"Get up, Phoenix. Get up or I swear to God I'm finna kill you and that bitch." She cocked the gun, and pulled back the hammer, ready to fire.

My dick popped out of Natalia's pussy with a loud suction sound. I jumped up with her juices dripping from the head of my dick, mixed with my own semen. Both my hands were raised and where Kamya could see them. A nigga was not trying to die for some ass today.

"Kamya, what the fuck is wrong wit you?"

Natalia rushed to the bed and wrapped a sheet around herself. "This makes no sense. We aren't doing anything wrong." The edges of her long hair was matted to the side of her forehead.

Kamya pointed the gun at her. "Bitch, if you don't shut up you're going to be the first family member that I kill. You got some nerve dropping into our lives and then taking him away from me. Y'all couldn't even wait for me to get out of the building before you were fuckin. You don't give a fuck about me, Phoenix!" While she kept the gun trained on Natalia, she said this last part screaming at me.

"Kamya, I don't know what to say. I guess, I'm sorry."

She shook her head. "No, you not Phoenix. All you care about is you. You don't care about me, or her, only yourself. It's all fun and games to you. You don't give a fuck about my feelings, or the way I feel about you. You took my fuckin virginity. You got me addicted to your ass, and this is how you treat me. It's not fair. It's just not fair Phoenix." She burst into tears.

Natalia wiggled out of the bed and fell to the floor out of sight. I didn't know what she had up her sleeves, but something wasn't right. Kamya acted as if she either didn't see her or didn't care. Her laser focus was on me.

"Baby, put that fuckin gun down. I do care about you, and how you feel about me. Me and her getting down ain't got nothing to do with my feelings toward you. You're my heart."

I didn't know how to play this situation. I had thoughts of rushing Kamya and taking the gun way from her ass. It would have been easy. The way she was holding it, a simple smack of the hand could have knocked it out of her grasp. But, a major part of me didn't want to hurt her. After all it was my fault that we were in this position. I didn't have any dick control. That was my problem. I had never been able to get control of that.

"If I was your heart ,Phoenix, you wouldn't be in here fuckin this bitch before I could even get out of the building. You don't love me. You never have. It's clear to me now. I swear I hate you right now."

10

Natalia grabbed a gun out of her purse and aimed it at Kamya. "Kamya, come on now. Drop that fuckin gun. I don't want to shoot you, but I will if I have to. Please don't make me do it."

Natalia stood there naked. She tapped her trigger and a red beam appeared from her pistol. The light pinned itself on Kamya's forehead.

"Take that shit off of her head, Natalia. It ain't finna come down to that. Now I fucked up. This is my fault. Y'all cease that shit."

Kamya shook her head. "Why should I, Phoenix? Why should I cease this? You're killing me. Whether this bitch puts a bullet in my head or not, you are still killing me. I can't handle what you are doing to me. You're making me weak. I am supposed to be able to depend on you for my shelter and my strength, but I can't. You're hurting me so bad."

I'd never seen Kamya so emotional. Her state of mind was effecting me in a major way. I felt like shit, lower then scum. I wanted to heal her in any way that I could. I honestly loved her with all of my soul. I didn't know that I meant as much to her as I really did. Now that I was conscious of her true feelings, I wished that I had handled things differently. I didn't know how for sure, but I felt that my understanding of Kamya was clearer now.

"Kamya, please, baby, put that gun down. This shit ain't finna go down like this."

"Listen to him, Kamya. Listen to him. Please. We're all family in this room. There is no need for blood shed. We can share him."

"Share him, bitch!" Kamya raised the gun and aimed it at Natalia.

Natalia fired two slugs from her gun. *Boom. Boom.*

Kamya flew into the night table and knocked the lamp off of the table. She fell to the ground and curled into a ball.

"Nooooooo!" I hollered and rushed to her side, knelt down and picked her up. Kamya lay weakly in my arms. There were two holes in her chest with blood gushing out of them rapidly.

"Baby. Baby. Fuck. What did you do, Natalia? What did you do?" I groaned, holding Kamya close.

Natalia got dressed. "Phoenix, we gotta get out of here. We gotta get her to a hospital. You know I didn't mean it. Had I not shot her she would have shot me. What would you have done?"

Kamya shook in my arms. She began to cough and tried to utter a few words, but no sound came out. Her eyes were bucked wide open.

"Phoenix, we need to get her to a hospital right away. Now! Get your ass up and get dressed."

***

I threw on my clothes as fast as I could. Then I scooped Kamya into my arms and headed down the back stairwell . Natalia was right behind me. When we got outside two of her body guards jumped out of her black hummer and rushed over to us. They spoke to her in Russian. She pointed at me, said something in her native language, and then one of the huge men was taking Kamya from my arms and placing her inside the hummer.

"Phoenix, come on, we'll take your truck. Let them get her to the hospital, this is the fastest way, come on we'll follow close behind.

Their hummer pulled off and stormed out of the parking lot. They placed a siren in the window. And then I understood why Natalia preferred for them to take her.

I got behind the wheel to my truck and started it and threw it in reverse. "You should have never shot her, Natalia. What the fuck was you thinking?"

I stepped in the gas. The truck began to move backward, but before I could get out of the parking spot, two black vans pulled in back of me and blocked my path. Fuck, they had me boxed in. The side doors to both vans swung open. I could see multiple masked gun men. Then the passenger to the first van jumped out, and the sight of Toya nearly caused me to have a heart attack.

She stood back. "Blow that muthafucka up. Kill him and that red bitch!" She ordered.

Ghost

Chapter 2

I couldn't believe my eyes at the sight of by daughter's mother. I was sure that Toya was dead. I had been sure that either Dragon, or Mikey had taken her out the game a few months prior. But no, here she was. Toya stood at the front of one of the vans, giving the order for her shooters to take my life. Mine, and my cousin Natalia's. I couldn't allow for that to happen.

"Phoenix get us the fuck out of here!" Natalia screamed. "I'm calling for back up right now." She assured, taking her phone out of her purse and texting like crazy.

Boom. Boom. Boom. Boom.

The windows of the truck exploded. Glass went everywhere, as more shots sounded.

Boom. Boom. Boom. Boom.

"Phoenix! What the fuck are you waiting on? Punch it!" Natalia hollered, falling to the floor of the truck.

I ducked down as far as I could and stepped on the gas. The truck sped backward and crashed into the two vans loudly. Sparks flew into the air. There was a loud sound of crunching metal. More shots came our way.

Boom. Boom. Boom. Boom.

The windshield of my truck was the next to go. Five bullet holes appeared in the glass and then it fell inward, and into my lap. My truck scraped its way free, knocking off one of the bumpers in the process. More rapid fire came my way before I punched the gas for the second time and shot across the parking lot at high speed. When I came the exit of the parking lot I stormed out of it, and into the street like a bat out of hell. Two cars that were coming from the intersection to the right of me slammed on their brakes and skidded a few feet, before crashing into the side of the truck knocking it sideways just a tad. The impact caused the airbags to deploy. The steering wheel looked like a white parachute. I expected the truck to be disabled when I stepped on the gas, but instead it lurched forward.

Natalia looked up from the floor, with a cut on the side of her forehead. A slight trace of blood dripped out of it, and down the side of her face. "Get us out of here Phoenix. If you don't we're going to die. My guys should be on there--."

Boom. Boom. Boom. Boom.

More tinkling of metal as the bullets landed in the paint of the truck. The back window exploded, and then the right side ones did the same. Natalia began to scream.

Zroom! *Errr-uh*! I found myself flying down Main street in an attempt to evade my attackers. I didn't understand what was going on. How was Toya coming at me so hard? And why? Was it because I'd taken her so-called first, true love Bryon out of the game? Because I had killed him for putting his hands on my daughter Shantê? And then her once in front of me?

Boom. Boom. Boom. Boom. Boom.

I swerved the truck from right to left, weaving in and out of the traffic. This was drama at its finest, heat at its maximum capacity. I looked in my rear view mirror and saw the two vans in hot pursuit. Toya sat in the passenger seat of one of them. She had an angry scowl on her face, I was able to see that after her van rolled past a street light, and the light illuminated the interiors of the truck.

I pushed my whip to forty miles an hour, then to fifty and then sixty. Made a violent right turn and nearly spun out of place. The steering wheel shook. I got on the entrance ramp for the highway and increased my speeds.

Looked into my rear view mirror and saw the two vans doing the same. What the fuck was their deal? Why was Toya having them to pursue me so forcefully? Was she aware that I'd just knocked off Dragon, one of the deadliest men in the south? The head of the Black Haven projects, and cousin to her so called first love? Or was she coming at me because after her mock kidnapping, I'd not come looking for her as hard as I had for our daughter Shantê when she had been snatched away?

Maybe it was all of those things, and then something else. Maybe Mikey, my long term right hand man turned enemy had gotten a hold of her and put a bunch of bullshit in her ear. Maybe he was trying to seek revenge through her because I had fucked his wife Alicia and gotten her pregnant. Or maybe Toya was salty because I was bringing another child into this world. A child that would have no strings or attachments to her and me as a collective.

The vans sped up on each side of me, though they were still back a nice ways. Then they were bussing again. Assault rifles shooting rapidly.

I reached under my seat. Grabbed the forty five automatic and handed it to Natalia. "You know how to shoot one of these?" I asked switching lanes.

She nodded, cocked the gun, and used the handle to knock out the remaining glass. Once she cleared a way for her arm to stick out of it, she was aiming back at them pulling the trigger.

Boo-wa. Boo-wa. Boo-wa. Boo-wa. Boo-wa.

I watched the scene unfold from my mirrors. One of the vans attempted to dodge the bullets. It swerved from right to left and crashed into the back of a Volvo station wagon . As soon as it crashed into the Volvo, a red car crashed into

17

the back of it knocking it forward, and within a matter of seconds there was a major car pile-up.

I floored the truck. Checking my rear view mirror for the other van. It was two lanes over storming. "Baby you see them mafuckas over there?" I pointed.

She followed the direction I was pointing. "Yeah I see 'em, and I got they ass too." She stuck the gun out of the truck and aimed. *Boo-wa. Boo-wa. Boo-wa. Boo-wa.* Her bullets struck the driver's side door, and the next thing I saw was a bunch of blood spray across the window as two holes appeared in the glass. The van sped up and wound up slamming into the back of a Fed Ex truck knocking it forward. The Fed Ex truck slammed on its brakes. Smoke drifted from the tires. The van smacked into it again, and wound up flipping over, and over, until it laid upside down on the side of the highway.

Natalia mugged the sight. "Come on baby. Let's get the fuck out of here. We gotta get to Mount Sinai right away. I had my men take Kamya to our private section of the hospital where she will get the best care possible, and we won't have to worry about the fuckin authorities." She placed the gun under her seat. "Phoenix I didn't want to shoot her. You know that right?"

I felt a lump in my throat. I wanted to believe that Natalia had no interest in hurting Kamya. That she'd not tried to kill her, but in all honesty I wasn't certain. I didn't know if her bullets were meant to kill, or to just simply stop Kamya from killing her or myself. I couldn't help but to be reminded of the fact that Natalia had taken her own mother out of the game. Either way, I could tell that my li'l cousin had been hurt severely. My last sight of her had been of a bloody mess. I was praying that she would pull through. I knew she was strong. She was a fighter. "Man, I don't wanna talk about that shit right now. You shot her, she was bleeding profusely. You need to pray that she pulls through. For the both of our sakes, Natalia." I glared at her.

She lowered her head. "Damn. I thought I was protecting you. I felt like she was getting ready to kill me first, and then you. Natalia looked so bewildered. I didn't mean to cause all of this heartache and pain. I swear I didn't." She exhaled loudly and looked up to me. "You don't hate me though right?"

I shook my head. "N'all, Natalia. I ain't got no hate in me for you. We already have way too many enemies. There is no room for us to hate each other. I just hope that Kamya is good." I switched lanes and took the next exit. I had to get off of the highway and switch whips again. I was sure that the shooting on the highway had been recorded by somebody, and there was only a matter of time before the police were hot on our tail . "Look Natalia we gotta switch this truck up. It's only a matter of time before the law is on our ass. You already know how they get down in Memphis." I reminded her.

She nodded. "Oh, don't worry, pull around this bend right here. We're going to meet up with a few of my guys on Martin Luther King Drive." She started to text on her phone again.

I followed her directives, missing Kamya. I was silently praying that my sins had not cost my cousin her life. She was only eighteen years old. She was my heart and soul. She came second to my daughter. There was nothing in this world that I wouldn't do for her. I meant that.

As soon as I turned on to MLK Drive, two black Hummers came out of nowhere. One of them waited until we stopped at a red light, before it pulled up alongside of my busted truck. Both of us jumped out of it and got into the Hummer.

"Sledge, you take that truck and get rid of it. You hear me?" She asked the big Russian, with the chubby, red face.

Sledge nodded, jogged to my truck, and got inside of it, and pulled off. He turned right at the corner and disappeared.

"Take us to Mount Sinai, and step on it." Natalia ordered the driver.

***

I felt sick on the stomach as I paced back and forth in the private waiting room of the hospital. My head was spinning like a tornado. Every time I breathed in, I felt like vomiting. Images of Kamya after she was shot were on replay in my mind. I couldn't block out the pain that was written all over her face. I knew that it was my fault. I'd played with her heart, taken her virginity, and gotten her to fall for me even though I knew I wasn't supposed to. We'd crossed more than the invisible line. We'd taken our forbidden love making to a whole other level where feelings had gotten involved. We had opened up feelings that were supposed to be nonexistent, I mean after all we were family. Nothing but bad things could ever come of our union. Man, I felt like an idiot. I missed her so much. Kamya was my baby. I needed her to pull through.

"Phoenix, can you sit down, damn, baby? You're driving me crazy with all of that fucking pacing. We've been waiting for five hours now, and that's all you've been doing. Please, come sit by me." She pleaded, tapping the cushions of the white leather sofa on the side of her.

Sitting was the last thing I wanted to do. 'What the fuck is taking them so long?" I wanted to know. "Why ain't they telling us anything?"

Natalia sighed and covered her pretty face with her hands. "I don't know, Phoenix, but I assure you that all of that pacing is no good for you. It's unhealthy. Now come and have a seat before you drive me just as crazy as you're on the path to becoming." She spoke weakly and patted the cushions again.

I waved her off. "Don't feel like sitting down. I wanna know what's good with by li'l cousin. That's my baby."

"Yeah. You mentioned that. Jesus. You still got me. I'm your cousin, too. Don't you care that I'm not doing so good mentally right now?" She asked standing up, and flipping her long, curly hair over her shoulder. After I ignored her question, she stepped into my line of pacing, stopping me in my tracks. "Well?"

I stopped and looked her over. "Natalia, don't do this shit right now, shawty. We're in a fuckin hospital waiting room. Kamya is fighting for her life and you're trying to turn things so that they're about you? Man, if you don't quit playin wit me I'ma choke yo li'l yellow ass out. Now sit yo ass down until them people call us. You hear me?"

She crossed her arms and stomped her right foot. "Fine. But, this stinks, Phoenix." She slumped on to the couch and began to pout like a li'l girl. Then she jumped up again.

I got ready to grab her by he throat. "What?"

She pointed. "They're coming."

I damn near snapped my neck to see what she was pointing to. A female doctor stepped out of the hallway and into the waiting room. She gave us a look of sympathy. "I'm sorry, we did everything that we could for her, but she'd lost so much blood. She was pronounced ten minutes ago. I'm so sorry." She tried to hand me a lap top so I could sign off as a witness to her death certificate.

I fell to my knees. Tears spilled out of my eyes. It didn't seem real. It couldn't be. Kamya couldn't be gone. No, not my baby. Not my heart and soul. I had done this to her. It was my fault. Had I never gotten involved with her she'd still be alive. I would never forgive myself. ''This can't be happening. She was only eighteen. She's my little cousin. I was supposed to protect her." I was in utter disbelief and feeling sick as a rabid dog.

Natalia stood biting her French manicured nails. She looked nervous and afraid. "Can you give us a minute, please. We need to discuss some family matters."

The Black, female doctor nodded, and walked away. She headed back the way she came. Before passing the nurses station the doctor stopped and began to chat with a white, female nurse as if this was just a normal part of her day. I wanted to kill both of them. I hated them for not feeling as low as I did.

Natalia dropped into the seat beside me. "I'm sorry Phoenix. Lord knows I'm so so sorry. You know I would have never killed her intentionally. I thought our lives were in danger. I need you to forgive me. Please." She lowered her face into her hands and began to sob.

I didn't know what to say to her at that moment. I hated her. Right then, I hated her for taking Kamya away from me, but I hated myself more. I hated myself more because I knew it was nobody's fault more than my own. I was devastated. So instead of wallowing beside Natalia, I stood up and walked over to the Black doctor. She was still talking to the white female nurse. "Excuse me, Miss?"

She turned to face me and smiled. Her face softened when she saw the look on my own. "Oh, hey there. How may I help you?"

"I wanna see my li'l cousin. I just need to see her one last time." I felt the tears streaming down my face. My heart felt like it was being ripped in two.

"Yes, Honey, sure. Right this way." She pointed down a white hallway that looked as clean as it could be. Two nurses walked down its corridor, conversing amongst themselves. She led the way.

I followed her. Natalia stayed a few paces behind me. I could tell that she was indecisive. She was unsure if it was her place to come and see Kamya's body for the last time, or not. I was so sick that I had no opinion about the matter at all. I knew that I needed to see her. I was dying to.

Two minutes later we were in the room. "Take as much time as you need, sir. And if I hadn't told you already, I am so sorry for your loss." the doctor said, before stepping out of the room and closing the door.

I walked over to the bed and stopped. I stood there for a minute looking down on her covered body. Then, I took a deep breath, and slowly pulled the sheet back until her face was revealed. As soon as I saw it, a flood of emotions overcame me. Our child hood flashed before me. All of the things we did as kids. The family gatherings, outings and the he love and affection we'd shared. And of course, all of the forbidden things. Kamya had always clung so tightly to me. Now she was gone. I felt horrible.

I slid part way into her bed, and pulled her into my arms, one last time I held her stiff body close to my own. I kissed the side of her forehead and rocked back and forth with her. "I love you, baby, and I'm so so sorry. I'm so so sorry Kamya. I fucked up. I fucked up real bad baby. Please forgive me for this shit. I wish I could have taken those bullets for you. I swear to God, I wish I could have." The next thing I knew I was breaking down like crazy. The more I cried, the colder my heart became.

Chapter 3
A month later...

I took the razor blade and chopped through the Rebirth. Separated it into four thick lines. Took the hundred dollar bill and rolled it up. Got it nice and tight before leaning my head sideways and tooting one of the lines hard. The drug blasted my brain. My depression subsided immediately. It was replaced with a feeling of euphoria. I could hear this happy music in my head that sounded somewhat like jazz mixed with R&B. My body felt numb, and relaxed. I felt like I was having an orgasm, while at the same time being on a rollercoaster. It was exhilarating.

The last four weeks had been the most difficult for me. Not a second went by that I didn't think about Kamya and how I had failed her. Her voice sometimes screamed at me in my head. It was like I could feel her touch. I found myself secretly going crazy. So much so that the only way I could combat my mixture of overpowering emotions was for me to experience the Rebirth. While it might not have been the smartest decision that I'd made, it was the most effective for me.

Smoke sat across the long table from me, counting a bundle of ten and twenty dollar bills that we'd just picked up from one of our many trap houses in the city. He pulled on his nose and looked across at me. "I still can't believe that bitch ,Toya, made it out of that situation alive. I heard she rolling with them Black Haven niggas real tough now. They honoring her like a fuckin queen. Can you believe that shit?" He asked, taking a stack of the cash and placing it inside of a money counter.

I grunted. "Fuck that bitch, Mane. We already know what it is, and because we do, shawty gotta be dealt wit.

It's fucked up cuz she's my daughter's mother, but she acting like she wanna play these grown ass war games, so it is what it is. I gotta buss her brain. I ain't got no other choice, my nigga." I tooted another line and felt my high intensify.

Smoke curled his upper lip. "Mikey think mafuckas forgot about his ass, too. Ever since this shit happened wit Toya, he been moving more and more of his traps over toward, and around Black Haven. I guess he's thinking he about to inherit that area, and all the money that comes along with it. That shit ain't finna happen. The Mound ain't enough. I don't give a fuck if we is making close to a million a day. That ain't enough for the Fam. I know you've already came to that conclusion. It's all about getting the whole crew rich now Phoenix. You done said that a few times yourself."

"You don't feed them lions they gone wind up putting you on the menu, homeboy. We gotta keep them animals fed. That's the way the game go. Can't nobody stand in the way of what we're trying to accomplish. That nigga, Mikey ain't on shit, Mane. It's time we start crushing him and his niggas on sight anyway. Matter of fact, fuck on sight, we about to go at that nigga, his crew, and anybody else in this city that looks to oppose the Duffle Bag Cartel. It's time to turn up. That's how the fuck I feel." I tooted my third line and sat back. My heart was beating fast as hell.

Smoke smiled and continued to count the money. He placed another stack on the money counter and started the machine. "Nigga, I love it when we talk this money shit. It gives me tingles all up and down my spine. But when you get to hollering about turning up, and bodying shit, that's when I get hyped. I get geeked up. I love that murder shit. I love wiping niggas out, Phoenix. I don't know why. That shit must be in my blood a something. I'm ready to waste some shit. Ready to torture a mafucka to death." He admitted, with a sinister look on his face. "How you wanna handle this shit wit Mikey? We gon rush in his shit and knock the meat out of his face or what?"

I laughed at the visual he gave me. I didn't think nothing would make me happier than being able to knock Mikey's brains out of his face. After being my right hand man for over ten years, now we hated each other more than cats hate dogs. "You talking like you got the jump in this nigga or something?"

"If you asking me if I know where he lay his head then that's a definite. I got a few bitches that been shacking up with him at his home away from the hood. He wouldn't be hard to touch. The only reason I ain't moved on his ass yet is because you ain't gave me the green light. You been saving him more then you know." He placed another stack of cash into the money counter and turned the machine back on.

I leaned forward and looked across the table at him. "Well, I'm letting you know this right now, that it ain't no more saving nobody. I'm on some no mercy shit. Any nigga. Any bitch. Anybody can get it, with no remorse. You ready to get on some killing shit, then let's lets get it!"

There were three knocks on the door, and then Natalia stuck her head in the room. Her long curly hair fell on each side of her face. She smiled at Smoke and glanced over. "Phoenix, can I talk to you for a minute? It's important."

I closed my eyes and allowed my system to absorb my high. My entire body felt as if it were tingling and being massaged at the same time. "Yeah, I'll be right there in a minute."

She nodded, and slowly closed the door. Before it closed all the way, she placed her phone to her ear and proceeded to talk into it.

"You better go see what she want. It might be something good. Shawty's ass is a gold mine." Smoke added.

I stood up. It boosted my high. I grabbed the pink Sprite off of the table and took a nice swallow from it. I could feel the medicine coursing down my throat. The feeling gave me the temporary shakes, and then my eyes were droopy. The Rebirth flowed through my system as if on a mission. By the time I stepped into the living room I was spacing.

Natalia saw me and hung up her phone. "Baby, so I got great news. Do you remember club Onyx that used to be on Addison Avenue?" She asked looking excited.

I nodded. Leaning like a muthafucka. "Yeah I remember it. What about it?"

"Well, I've been in talks with the property owners of that building for a few weeks now trying to see what they wanted to do with it, and guess what?"

"What?"

"We own it. Well, I mean I bought it for you, so you own it. I already got a bunch of bitches lined up ready to audition for a spot inside of it. I wanna let you pick out every last female. Anything that will make you happy."

I didn't know what to say. Ever since Natalia had killed Kamya, she'd been trying her best to do whatever it took to stay on my good side. The latest purchase of the strip club was a blind side to me. I didn't even know what had made her go ahead and snatch it off the market. "That's what's up, Natalia. I appreciate you, but you should know you ain't gotta keep doing li'l shit like this. Kamya is gone, shawty. We gotta get over that shit. Me and you are cool.

We straight." I took a long swallow from the bottle again. "You hear me?"

She ran her fingers through her hair. "I feel like shit. Still. I don't know what to do to get over this. I know how much she meant to you. I can only imagine how you see me right now. I think I would hate me right now. I'm just being honest." She stepped to me and laid her forehead on my chest.

I wrapped my arm around her and held her for a minute and inhaled the scent of her perfume. She hugged my waist. "Damn, Natalia. Every time I try and get over Kamaya's death you keep on bringing me back to round zero. I loved our cousin. If I keep dwelling on what happened to her, it's gone be fucked up for the both of us. Now, we need to let this shit go."

"I know, and I am trying so hard. Honestly. Every time I close my eyes she is all that I see. I still hear the shots, see the blood and I can see her going down. I wish I could take away the past. I wish we had never done what we had. Now she's gone." She fell into my chest and began to sob. This had been damn near an everyday thing since Kamya's death. Natalia seemed to be taking it harder than me. Well, at least, that's how it appeared on the outside. Inside I was just as fucked up. I was so thankful for the Rebirth because it allowed for me to feel numb more than not, and the feeling of numbness is what I needed to feel.

I rubbed her back, pulled on her hair so she could lean her head back and rested my cheek against hers. "We said we were gonna to get through this together right ,baby? Just you and me. Right?"

Natalia nodded. "Yeah. We did. I'm so sorry, Phoenix. I just know that she was a hell of a sweet heart and I took her away from you. Can you honestly say that you'll ever forgive me?"

I continued to hold her. I really didn't know the answer to that. Deep down in the pit of my heart was hatred for what she'd done to Kamya. I wanted to body her ass, and I didn't think I would ever get over that feeling. The Rebirth helped a lot with my urges to slay her, but at the same time I didn't know how long those feelings would stay suppressed. Natalia was trying to accomplish so much for me. I knew that through her, and her connections, not only could I advance in the game, but I could conquer it. Even though I was still pissed, and her life was in jeopardy when it came to the monster inside of me, I couldn't let that be known. I was smarter than that. Taking a step back, I brushed her long hair out of her pretty face, I rubbed the sides of her cheeks with my thumbs. "Baby, listen to me and listen good. I love you, and I forgive you. Everything is going to be okay as long as you keep doing what you're doing. Let's take all of that hurt, and pain and use it to get rich. I want my own empire as a man. Help me to get that. I need you. Do you hear me, baby?"

She nodded her head. A lone tear fell from her left eye. "Do you really love me, Phoenix? Like really and truly love me?"

"Of course, I do. You go hard for me. I see that. I gotta rider standing right in front of me. Me and you are all that we have. You understand me?"

She smiled, and sniffled. "I do, and I love you too, Phoenix. I love you with all of my heart. I would never do anything to hurt you. I just want to make you as happy as you make me by just being here. Can you kiss me?" She stepped in her tippy toes and brushed her nose against my own.

The scent of her perfume drifted up my nose. Natalia smelled good. She always did. I pulled her soft body into my embrace. Kissed her lips, licked them, then sucked first the bottom, and then the top. Her tongue lashed out at me. I caught it and sucked it. After that I kissed her lips some more. We went from just kissing to tonguing each other hungrily. I gripped that plump ass and breathed into her mouth with short, labored gasps of air.

Natalia's breathing was just as ragged. She moaned. "I want you so bad, Phoenix. Can we? I mean just for a few minutes. Please. Anything that will take us out of this funk." She groaned, leaning her neck backward to look up at me.

I sniffed up and down her neck, sucked all over it, and bit into it. Without giving it a though I picked her ass up and Natalia wrapped her legs around me. Then we were kissing again. My dick was harder than a gangster rapper. It was throbbing in my pants as I kissed Natalia's pussy. She and I hadn't had sex since Kamya had passed away. I didn't think that either of us could go there mentally. I knew it was hard for me too. But now I was feening for her cat. It was always so wet, hot and tight. I needed a shot of it. The Rebirth had me ready to go. I held her against the wall. "You want me to fuck this pussy Natalia, huh baby?"

"Hell, yeah Phoenix. Right here if you want too." She wiggled out of my embrace and started to open my pants. My dick was so hard that as soon as she unbutton them my piece head stuck straight up, and out at her. Her fist wrapped around it. "I want you to fuck me right now Phoenix. I'm hurting."

Ghost

Chapter 4

Natalia dropped to her knees and stroked my piece in her little fist. Her tongue ran across her juicy lips. "I need you Phoenix. I need to know that you don't hate me. You haven't touched me since that accident happened." She continued to stroke me. Her speed increased. Then her fist parked at the base of my pipe. She slid her mouth over the top of the head and sucked hard. Her tongue traced circles around and around it, before she began to deep throat me like a porn star.

I grabbed a hand full of her hair. Tangled my fingers inside of it and rested with my back against the wall. "Damn Natalia. Un. Fuck. Just shut up. Uh. Quit talking bout that shit. Uh. Mmm. Shit. Yeah. Get me ready to hit this pussy."

As Natalia continued sucking me her mouth was so wet that I could hear the slurping sounds coming from it. She popped it out and stroked it up and down. "I'm sorry baby. I'm so sorry. I just want you to fuck me so bad. I miss this forbidden dick of yours. Need to feel it inside of me." She sucked me back into her mouth, ran her hand down her stomach, and up under her short skirt. I heard the elastic to her panty's waistband pop. Her fingers slid lower, then she moaned around my dick head loudly. "Unnnn." Her head bobbed up and down.

My eyes rolled into the back of my head. The feeling got better and better. It had been so long since we had gotten down that I didn't want to waste my first nut in her mouth, especially so swiftly. I pulled her up by her hair and pushed her against the wall and sucked on her neck. "You miss this taboo shit don't you? You want a piece of the family back in this pussy Natalia?"

"Yes! Fuck yes!"

I sucked down her neck, cupped her breasts inside of her blouse and sank lower. In my rush to get closer to Natalia I yanked the blouse over her head and tossed it to the floor. Within seconds I was sucking and biting along the expanse of her stomach. I could feel her shivering

"I love you Phoenix. I swear to God I do baby. I love you so freaking much." She spread her thighs.

My head went under her skirt. The scent of her arousal was nice and heavy. I inhaled deeply, licked the front of her panties and sucked on one of the thick lips. To slow things down, I rubbed up and down her groove with two fingers, before pulling the lace material of her boy shorts to the side. Natalia's yellow pussy lips popped out fully engorged and covered with dew. My tongue attacked the juices. I spread her sex wide with both thumbs, before sliding my tongue up and down her crease. Her clit was poked out the top of her goods like a small pinky. It brushed against my nose while my tongue worked in and out of her body.

She grabbed the sides of my head and humped into my face. "Eat me cuz. Uhh. Eat me. Eat yo baby. Uhhhhh fuck, Phoenix." Natalia stepped on her right toes, and spread her thighs further bussing her pussy open.

Two fingers slid into her hole. Her juices ran into the palm of my hand and dripped off of my wrist. My lips trapped her clit and sucked hard, while my tongue went from side to side flickering.

She humped faster. "Uhhh. Uhhh. I'm finna cum Phoenix. Oh my God. I'm finna cummmmmmmmmmm! Uhhhhh-shiiiiiiiiit!" She screamed, humping into my face. My cheeks were smeared with her secretions, but I kept on sucking at her clit until she was shaking against me, and

34

cuming hard. Her knees buckled. She fell to the floor in the front room.

I flipped her ass over and sucked on her ass cheeks and opened them. I licked up and down her crack, tracing a circle around her pink rose bud. Then I was eating that pussy from the back while she knelt on all fours, breathing heavy. Natalia was so thick, and yellow. Them fat ass cheeks jiggled with each movement, along with her thighs. She rested her face on the carpet and moaned over and over. Her hand snuck between her thighs. Played with her pussy while I ate it and sucked her greasy fingers at the same time. "Fuck me now Phoenix. Put your dick in me. We're family." She spread her kitty lips with two fingers, exposing her inner pink.

I knelt behind her and stroked my dick up and down as I rubbed all over that juicy booty, squeezed it, and smacked it twice, hard.

She arched her back. "Uhhh. Please fuck me, daddy. I need you right now."

My head ran up and down her sex lips. She was leaking so bad that it ran down her thighs. I licked up as much as I could. Then, I was fitting my dick into her forbidden pussy again. I pushed forward and continued sinking deeper and deeper. Her hole swallowed me inch by inch. It got hotter as hotter the further I went. My balls rested against her pussy lips, and my abs were on her ass cheeks. Her walls throbbed around my pole.

"You're in me again. You're in me again. Uh. Yes. Now fuck me, cuz, as hard as you can."

She didn't have to tell me twice. I grabbed her hips, pushed her forward, and pulled her all the way back hard. Her ass crashed into my stomach. Her thighs jiggled.

She yelped. "Yes!"

As I watched my dick go in and out of Natalia, the sight of her pussy lips opening and closing around it egged me on. I became obsessed with the scent of us. She smashed back into my lap over and over, taking my huge dick like a champ, even though it was stuffing her li'l tight pussy. Her titties bounced up and down on her chest. I placed my hand in her back of her neck and forced her face into the carpet. I began fucking her so hard that I couldn't help making a few sounds of my own. There was nothing like that forbidden pussy. It just felt different. My dick loved it. I smacked her on that juicy ass. *Smack*!

"Uh! Shit! Phoenix." She crashed backward into me faster and faster. "Cum in me, Phoenix. Cum in me. Uh. Uh. Uh. Uh. Ooo. Cum in my pussy, daddy. It's yours! It's yours! Tell me I'm yo baby! Tell me!" She hollered.

Smoke stepped into the hallway, catching us in the act. He bucked his eyes. He placed his fist in front of his mouth, mouthing the words *damn*. He looked down to Natalia's thrusting ass and grabbed his piece through his pants.

I smacked her ass. "You're my baby. I'm daddy. I'm yo daddy. Call me Taurus when I hit this pussy."

Natalia shivered. "Aw fuck! Shut up. Daddy. Shut up. You gon make me cum. You gon make me cum." She slammed backward harder and harder.

The high we were on was feeling so good that all I could do was close my eyes and absorb the sex bout. "Call me Taurus. Call me Taurus, Natalia. I'm daddy. Daddy finna cum in this pussy. You my baby."

She screamed. "Cum in me ,daddy. Cum in yo baby girl! Aww, shit I'm cumming hard dadddddeeeee!" She smashed backwards into me, cumming hard over my pole.

This sparked my own orgasm. As soon as I felt it skeeting off inside of her, I pulled him out and started to jerk him up and down. Nut flew out of the head and landed on her rounded ass cheeks. Natalia opened her legs wide so I could cum all over her slightly parted pussy lips. She reached under herself and rubbed the cum into her pussy, and the skin of her ass.

I scooted around on my knees and fed her my dick and watched her suck me like a champion. Her naturally blue eyes were peering into my brown ones. Natalia was a bad bitch. I couldn't deny that fact. If I wasn't careful I could find myself becoming addicted to her li'l ass because she was just as obsessed with that forbidden shit as I was. Our DNA appeared to be fucked up.

Smoke slipped into the bathroom and closed the door. I could only imagine how geeked up the sight of Natalia had gotten him. From his view from the hallway he would have been able to see her taking a smooth dicking. He already acted as if he had a thing for her, low key.

***

Ten minutes after our fucking ceased, we wound up in the shower, washing each other's bodies. After the shower we cuddled up in the bed. She hugged up to my body naked, and wrapped her thick, left thigh around my waist. I could feel her hot pussy on my hip. My hand cupped her ass and squeezed it. I kissed her forehead then trailed my fingers down in between her crack and played with the lips. I loved playin with Natalia's pussy. It gave me a sense of power.

She kissed my nipple. "Baby, I'm ready for you to go hard. I'm ready for you to be more than what my mother wanted my father to be, and I'm going to help you."

I smiled. Now she was talking about that shit that I wanted to talk about. It could have been easy for me to just sit back and let her do everything, I wasn't on that. I was still my own man. I'd been grinding in the slums my whole life and nothing had ever been handed to me, and I wasn't expecting it to be now. The man, and hustler in me needed to grind for my shit. I needed to know that at the end of the day that I was the king of everything that was brought into fruition. The most important thing was that I never wanted to give Natalia a place to make herself feel like she made me. Fuck that. I was self-made and self-invested. "Baby, you already know how I get down. I'll accept your help but only to a certain degree. I gotta do this shit on my own, with you having by back though. You feel me?"

She kissed my nipple again, licking at it with her tongue. "Baby I'll do whatever you want me to do, I'm rich. Or shall I say we're already rich. Because of my parents we'll never be broke. But I understand that you want your own. That's so sexy to me. I wish I could marry you Phoenix. I ain't trying to fuck wit no other man but you. Every time you're eleven inches deep in my pussy it just gives me chills. Then when you was telling me to call you that name. Fuck, it was driving me crazy. You're turning me out, and I love it." She kissed her way down my stomach, rubbing all over the prominent muscles. Her hand sunk lower and stroked my dick.

Two fingers slipped into her from the back. They went in and out of her hole. My wrist rested on her ass crack. I could feel myself getting hard. This is what that forbidden shit did to a nigga. "Natalia, I want the South. I'm talking from Texas to Florida, I want this shit. What you gon do to help me with that?"

She shivered as my fingers went as deep into her body as they could. Natalia turned more on her side and opened her thighs wider. "I want you Phoenix. I want you to marry me. For you to be any husband. I don't care about the laws in America. We'll go out of the country if we need to. I just want to possess a part of you. Is that so wrong?" She asked, straddling my waist. She laid her chest on mine. Natalia reached behind her and grabbed a hold of my dick. The big head throbbed over the gates to her garden. She peeled her lips apart, and it sank into her like a hot knife into a stick of butter. "Mmm. Daddy."

I shook my head, held her hips and groaned. "N'all baby. It's only right that you wanna possess a part of me. But you gotta earn that. I can only cross over to you after I become a king of my own throne. You understand that?"

Natalia nodded, and slid backward, inhaling my dick with her pussy. I could literally feel the ridges inside of her walls. "I'll do anything." She popped her hips. Fuckin me slowly with her blue eyes looking into mine. I could tell that she was experiencing a twinge of pain. Her bottom lip quivered

I bounced her up and down. "You gotta follow my rules. You gon fall under me. I'm daddy. I'm king. I run this shit. You got that baby girl?" I bounced her faster and faster. My fingers gripped her ass. I pulled them apart so far that her ass hole was visible.

"Yes daddy. Yes. Yes. I'll listen. Baby girl will listen. Just tell me. Tell me. Tell me what to do. Tell me. Unnnn. You run dis shit. You run dis shit. Fuck baby." She bounced higher and higher, riding me faster and faster with her head thrown back. Natalia's perfect breasts shook in her chest. Her long hair fell over shoulder and all the way down to her stomach. The feel of her pussy sucking at me was enough to drive he crazy but I had to stay the course. Keep my foot on her neck, so to speak. Cousin or not.

"Get me right Natalia. Get me right, and you can possess me. I'll. Marry. You. But my kingdom. Uh fuck. My kingdom. Comes first. You. Hear. Me?"

"Yes. Yes. Yes. Yes. Uhhhhh. Fuck yes. Daddy. Daddy. Uh fuck yo baby girl, daddy. Ooo. Ooo. Shit! I'm cumming! I'm cumming so hard!"

I dug deeper inside her, making her impale herself on it. She slid all the way down on it and bit into my neck and sucked hard. I came, spewing my seed deep into her womb, again and again. My dick felt sore as soon as I splashed.

She laid her head in my chest and worked her pussy muscles, milking me. "I'ma get this club up and running for you Phoenix. Then, I'll order another shipment of the Rebirth. If you need more men I'll get them for you too. The sooner you conquer what you're trying to, the sooner I can have you for myself. Is that right?"

"I want the South for now. Help me to get this, and I'm yours. You'll have your kingdom. I'll make sure of that. You just do your thing, and I'll do what I have to do. Bank on it." She closed her eyes and began riding me hard, with her mouth wide open.

I couldn't help but to have money signs going through my mind. I was sure that Natalia was going to be my way in. My connect. My yellow brick road to the kingdom that I knew I deserved.

Chapter 5

"Yeah, Phoenix, I know you gon appreciate this shit. One of my li'l hoes told me that this li'l nigga admitted to her that he took part in that shooting when yo truck got shot up last month. The bitch ain't gon lie either. She been Orange Mound since she came into this world. Her mother gave birth to her right in the projects." Smoke laughed and mugged the nigga that was seated, and duct taped to the chair.

"I ain't have time to question him and all that good shit. I figured you'd like to do that honors." He knelt and picked up a book bag that was full of utensils. Then tossed it to me.

I caught it. We were in the basement of one of our traps right outside of the Mound. I wanted to get to the bottom of things. I needed to know how Toya had gotten so plugged to the point that she was able to give orders to a bunch of niggas that was ready to commit murder for her at her order. A lot of shit had changed within a year, and I felt like I was behind and even slipping a li'l bit. There were four of our Cartel animals in the basement alongside me and Smoke. I figured that it was important for me to set the standard of how our shit was gon roll from here on out, so once Smoke hit me up and told me the circumstances, I'd arranged for him to have our looniest of hittas present. When it came to a Cartel, as the head you had to be the deadliest. Every man was a born head, so you never knew when one of your animals would try and take your slot. The crazier, more sadistic you were in their presence, the less likely the chances of one of your soldiers rising up against you.

I walked in front of the taped bandit, and snatched the tape off of his mouth, then I slammed the book bag on the table next to him. "We gon do this real nice and sweet, my nigga. I ain't about them games, you feel me?"

This nigga mugged me and turned up his nose. He was dark skinned, with gray eyes and dread locks that fell to his lap. Both of his wrists, and ankles were duct taped to the chair. "Say, Mane, I don't know why da fuck y'all got me down hurr, potna, but dis ain't what it is. Y'all need to let me da fuck go right now. Dess what dat iz."

I stepped in front of him and crouched down so that we were eye to eye. "You know who I am, Playboy?"

He sucked his gold teeth. "Yeah I know who you iz. What about it?" He had one if those I don't give a fuck demeanors. I was about to find out real quick how long that would last.

"You know Toya?" I asked, patient.

He laughed. "Nigga who don't. Shawty a jump off for the mob. Shat? Dess what dis all about? A bitch? Y'all definitely got me fucked up, Potna."

That made me laugh. "What type of pull shawty got over you and yo niggas to have y'all shooting at me?"

"Mane, I don't know what you talking bout. I ain't shot at nobody. My niggas ain't either. But, if you mafuckas don't let me go soon, we gon change all of that. Black Haven won't take too kindly to mafuckas kidnapping one of they Capos. We likely to blow this whole Project off the face of the earth. You niggas don't know what y'all getting y'all selves into."

"Oh, is that right?" I asked.

"That's muthafuckin right." He returned.

Smoke rummaged around inside of the bag and came out of it with a hammer. "Here you go, Boss." He handed it to me.

"Bruh, scoot this fuck boy to the table, and place that hand on that mafucka. Spread them fingers for me." I ordered Smoke.

"Y'all heard the Homie. Hurry the fuck up. This Duffle Bag bidness." Smoke snarled, mugging our prisoner. "We gon see if you be talking that tough shit in a minute, Mane. We Orange Mound over here, cousin. Fuck you Black Haven niggas." Smoke spat and pulled his nose.

"Black Haven to the death of me, homeboy. I don't give a fuck what you niggas finna do. Bury me a G, my nigga."

Our hittas forced his chair closer to the table. My niggas untapped his right hand and slammed it on the table. Two of them worked together to space his fingers apart for me.

I took a nail out of the bag and placed the point of it over his pinky finger. "How Toya got so much power, now? Who ordered for you to take me out, nigga? Who calling the shots?"

"Mane, fuck you. I ain't got shit to say." He snapped.

I laughed. "Aiight, fuck nigga, we finna see. Tape his mouth back." I waited until Smoke replaced the tap, then took the hammer and slammed it as hard as I could into the nail driving it through his pinky finger and into the table. Once the nail sunk part way into the table, I hammered it the rest if the way while he screamed at the top of his lungs into the tape.

Smoke busted up laughing and clapped his hands together. "Hell yeah. That's the shit I'm talking about. This fuck nigga screaming like a bitch now." He pointed. "Look at him."

Dude tried his best to hop up and down in his chair. Blood gushed out of his pinky. It ran along the table. Sweat appeared on the side of his face, and along the edges of his hairline. Snot oozed out of his nose.

"You ready to talk, nigga? Huh?" I ripped the tape off of his mouth. I already had the next nail lined up, ready to be inserted into his ring finger.

"Fuck you, nigga. Ain't no hoes over here, Potna. It's Black Haven to he death of me. I bleed for my deck. I--."

Bam.

The nail pierced through his next finger. It stopped at the bone. I raised the hammer way over my head and brought it down as hard as I could. His finger looked smashed. The nail caused it to fold inward. *Bam.* Another hit and blood spurted into the air.

"Ahhh! Ahhh! You bitch ass nigga. I'ma kill you, Phoenix. I'ma kill you, on everythang I love, Mane!"

I lined the next nail up over his middle finger. "How Toya got all that power like that, Mane? Who she getting it from?" I asked in a voice that was deadly calm.

Tears ran down his eyes. "Man, fuck Toya, Playboy. I don't fuck wit dat bitch like dat. She ain't calling shots over me. Ain't no hoe gon ever be able to so that." His chest heaved up and down. More sweat poured from his face. It caused his neck to glisten.

"Who gave them orders for you to hit up my ride? My cousin was in that car, nigga. You almost killed shawty. Some mafucka gotta pay for that. If you don't wanna tell me what's good then I don't have a problem letting you take the wrap until I get to the bottom of it." *Bam.*

"Ahhh! Son of a....Ahh!" He started to shake like crazy.

Bam. Bam. Bam.

I made sure that the nail was planted all the way into the table like I'd done the other ones. The table was a bloody mess. The sight excited me. I was praying that he kept his mouth closed. The more he did, the longer I would be able to inflict bodily harm on his ass. I grabbed the next nail and lined it up over his index finger. "You got something you wanna say to me?"

He clenched his gold teeth together. "Argh-ahhhhh! I hate that Toya bitch! She got my brother, Bryon, killed. Nigga everybody in Black Haven know that you the one that killed him. Not only did she tell us, but ya right hand Mikey called a truce and told us what it was too. Say you was on some jealous shit. Her and him been fuckin around, she was fuckin wit him and Bryon at the same damn time. I told my brother them Orange Mound hoes ain't no good. You might not have seen it, but that bitch pregnant wit his seed, nigga. They both rotten, and they gon murder yo ass, you and these pussy niggas in yo Cartel. You need to let me go. I'm the reason yo daughter still alive right now. Me and only me. Mikey gave me the order to smoke her, but I stalled. Even that bitch Toya was good wit it. She say all that li'l girl do is remind her of you anyway." His blood began to drip off of the table. It created a puddle on the cement floor.

I couldn't believe what I was hearing. It sounded like he was saying that Mikey had been fucking off with Toya all along. If that was the case then how the fuck could he have been salty that I was screwing Alicia? That was mind boggling to me.

"For the record, nigga, the only way we knew that you was gon be at that hotel was because somebody in your outfit tipped us off. Every nigga that's rolling wit you, aint really riding for you, if you get my drift." He closed his eyes and took a deep breath.

I looked over the five killas that were in the room wit me. My mouth got dry. I felt a chill travel down my spine. "I thought Mikey was beefing hard wit you niggas out in Black Haven? Dragon ain't fuck wit that nigga. What, since he gone now, y'all jamming wit his enemies?"

"Man, Dragon ain't have us eating the way he should have been. All that fool cared about was himself and his inner circle, which consisted of his relatives. I could barely expect to make two gees a week under him. But wit Mikey, bruh, come right in on bidness. The nigga threw me a brick of some Russian shit off the rip. In two weeks, I made a hunnit thousand, and that's what all of Black Haven is reporting. Mafuckas ready to kill for him more than they were for Dragon. That fool constantly building up his army. It ain't sweet." He winced in pain and started to shake.

Smoke mugged him and then me. "Man, kill this nigga, Phoenix. His pussy ass look like he on his way out anyway. Then we can finish this fuck nigga, Mikey, and take over Black Haven." He said, looking dude over closely.

"What's the game plan, homeboy?" I asked, pointing the hammer in his face.

"Don't know nothin about no game plan. I just handle bidness when they tell me to. That's above my pay grade."

I shook my head. "Nall, nigga, you lying. You know way too much to not know what their next move is going to be. I can't buy that shit." I took the next nail and smashed it through his index finger. Without even blinking, I beat it until his finger was flattened into the table. More blood gushed from it and I smiled. Zero fucks given.

He fainted. Dude was snoring loud as hell. I couldn't believe it. That was the first time I'd seen anything like that happen. It was fascinating.

Smoke stepped forward and spit into his hand, raised it in the air and smacked ole dude so hard that he split his nose. "Wake yo bitch ass up!" He roared.

The dude jolted awake. He opened his eyes wide, looked down at the condition of his fingers and hollered out in pain. "This some bull shit. This some bull shit. I can't take this shit no more."

Smoke grabbed him by the face. "Tell him what he needs to know. You wasting our muthafuckin time."

He shook his head. "I don't know what their next move is. I swear I don't. All I know is that they're out for your blood. They want you gone. You and your daughter. Mikey got Black Haven. He coming for the Mound next. Believe that shit. You bitch niggas need to have mercy on me and kill me where I sit. I'll see you pussies in hell." He turned his head upward and spit into Smoke's face.

I took the hammer and swung it as hard, and as fast as I could. The pounder caught him on the side of the jaw. He hollered. I swung the hammer again and implanted it into the middle of his forehead. I pulled it out and slammed it into him again.

He tried to talk. Blood gushed from his face. It ran out of his mouth, and from his fingers. The floor looked like paint had been spilled. It smelt like copper in the basement.

Smoke yanked the hammer from me after wiping the captive's spit off of his cheek and began beating him over the head with it relentlessly. His chair fell over, yet his hand remained planted to the table. It was a crazy sight. Smoke went nuts. Pounding harder and harder. Faster and faster. When it was all said and done, he left the basement a mess.

He'd beat the dude's head in so bad that it turned to mush. I'd never seen somebody get beat with a hammer so badly. After Smoke finished, he stood over the man with his chest heaving up and down. Blood dripped from the tool. I could see little pieces of flesh scattered about the basement.

"It's time this Cartel murder its way through Memphis because we've got bigger things at stake. You mafuckas keep fuckin wit me and we about to have the whole south. Trust that." I looked around at each man.

They nodded their heads and kept mugs on their faces. Their eyes told me that they were ready for the unknown. This war shit was alluring to them, like it was to me. There was no way that I was about to just let Mikey inherit Black Haven. That piece of land was a gold mine. In the game, whoever had the most money, had the most power. Money gave you power, and power gave you the right connections. Connections helped you to set your plans in motion. Plans helped you to strategize in such a way to conquer and win in the game. I wanted and needed for me and my cartel to be at the top of the food chain of the South. I wanted to start with the South because it is what I knew.

After that was conquered, we would venture into the northern hemisphere of the country. But, just like with anything else in life, you had to crawl before you were able to walk . Respecting the game would be hard for me because I saw everybody in the game as a threat, or an enemy. I knew that on the road to riches a lot of bodies would be left behind. My main focus was that my own body and those of my bloodline were not left a part of the heap of carcasses that was to be. It wasn't gon be easy getting to where I needed to be. Nothing worth having ever was. I was on a lethal mission and refused to be denied.

Chapter 6

Smoke rolled up the tinted windows of the 1984 Chevy Caprice classic two days later. He slid a pair of black leather gloves on his hands. It was nine o'clock at night and drizzling outside. We were both higher than gas prices.

Smoke sniffled and pulled his nose. "I don't give a fuck no more Phoenix. Niggas playin' a dirty game out here, Boss. The only way ma'fuckas gon start respecting this Duffle Bag shit is if we start bringing that noise to every ma'fucka that act like they above getting scorched with this heat. It's Orange Mound a nothin, my nigga. To the dirt wit this shit, Mane. Memphis belongs to us." He threw the car in drive and pulled down the alley and made a right turn at the end of it. He eased out, and parked the car in front of The Tavern, a spot that t was known in Black Haven for some of the best burgers and fries in town. It seemed like once we entered on to the street it started raining like crazy.

I fixed the half mask over my face and pumped the big Marburg shotgun. It had five shots, and I planned on using every single slug. I was drunk off of that Lean and drooping from a gram of the Rebirth. I was in kill mode.

Smoke nodded his head toward The Tavern. "My sources tell me that this bitch finna have a few of Mikey's soldiers in this bitch. I heard it was ma'fuckas that's on his front line." He adjusted his rear view mirror. "Our fellas just pulled up too. We about to have a shotgun party. This bitch finna go down in history." He grabbed his heat off of the back seat and rolled a Donald Trump mask down his face.

I chuckled. This fool always had to go above and beyond to be different, or to make a statement. That was funny to me. "Let's go in here and handle this bidness." I pushed open the passenger's door to the car and stepped into the rain and took a quick look along the curb at the other cars that were lined up in front of the establishment, and all the ones across the street. I was unsure of how many people were going to be in here but from what I could see it appeared to be a lot. I didn't give a fuck. I had five shots in the shotgun, and about thirty more rounds in my pocket.

I waited until one of our hittas that was also masked with a Donald Trump face, pulled open the door to the Tavern. He pumped his shotgun and stepped to the side.

I ran up the eight steps. As soon as I got close to the door's entrance I heard the sounds of Moneybagg spitting through the speakers. I rushed inside of the bar. There were about twenty dudes nodding their heads with bottles of liquor in their hands. They were crowded around a pool table. A bunch of females walked to and from. I stopped ten feet in front of the door and aimed at the crowd of men. "Duffle Bag, Bitches!"

Bloom! Bloom! Bloom! Bloom!

My bullets exploded necks and knocked the bodies they crashed into backward. Throwing them over the pool table in a bloody mess that excited me.

Bloom!

Another shot that exploded the back of a head. I knelt down and reloaded while my cartel went to work.

The crowd began to holler, scream, and disburse. They were tripping over each other trying to make their grand escape. It was almost comical. Smoke joined in on the firing.

Bloom. Bloom. Bloom. Bloom.

I stood up and gazed at all of the bodies strewn across the floor. Each had either one or two big holes inside of them. The room smelled like gun powder and burnt pieces of flesh. It was the scent of war and conquering. I began firing, hitting random targets. There weren't many left. I avoided the women as best I could. Three minutes after we came into The Tavern on bidness we were out, back in the whips, and headed for the Mound.

***

That night, as I was showering away the day's bloody events, Natalia came into the bathroom, and stepped into the shower with me, after pulling off her tee shirt. Her pretty titties bounced on her chest. The circular, brown nipples stood at attention like they needed to be sucked. She took a bunch of suds off of my back and rubbed them into her breasts. Then her arms slid around my waist. "I missed you today daddy. I been thinking about you all day long." She kissed all over by back, then trailed her small hand around until she was gripping my piece. Her thumb played over the head. In an instant I was rock hard, and she was stroking it. "Let me suck this." She turned me around by using my tool.

The water spattered on to the side of my face as I looked down on her, and slowly slid into her mouth. Fucking into it slowly at first, and then gradually building speed. My fingers roamed through her naturally curly locks. Gripped them, I used them to get the best benefits of her sucking.

Natalia slurped, then gagged when she took me deep. She pulled it out and licked all over the head before she started sucking it again. Her fingers crept between her legs. She peeled her lips apart, and slid her middle finger into her juicy box, jamming it in and out.

It felt so good, I found myself groaning. My eyes rolled backward, and my abs tensed up. Natalia rubbed all over them while she sucked me. Then she popped me out of her mouth and bent over holding onto the wall in the shower. The water cascaded off of those fat ass cheeks until they were glistening.

I knelt behind her and opened her ass cheeks up, licking her crinkle. I forced my tongue as far inside of her as it could reach, while I rubbed her juicy, hairless, yellow pussy that was hot as fresh baked bread.

"Yes, daddy. Yes. Ooo. Eat me. It feels so good. Eat me Phoenix. Uh! It feels so good." She spaced her feet further apart.

My face rested on her ass cheeks. I held them apart while my tongue went crazy. I was eating that ass like it was my last meal. Her clit came further and further from between her lips. It poked out like a mini Vienna sausage. I diddled it with thumb, then I was fingering her while I ate that fat ass booty. Her cheeks clenched around my tongue.

She humped backward into my face. "Unn daddy. Unn. Unnnn. I'm finna. I'm finna. Ahhh shit!" She purred.

I started sucking her clit and drinking her savory flavors. Her juices trailed from my lips, and down over my Adam's apple. Natalia's pussy was always wet and ready to go. I loved that shit about her.

I stood up. "Open that ass for daddy baby." I squirted a decent amount of body wash into the palm of my hand and started stroking my dick with it. I wanted to fuck Natalia's ass. I was feening too She was so fucking thick, and righteous. Any female that was as strapped as she was needed to have that ass hit. Damn our relation. I had to have some of that. The way my dick was jerking up and down told me just that.

She held them apart and laid her chest on the wall. "Do it daddy. Do it. You can have me anyway that you want me. Just as long as you have me. I'm yours. I'm your bitch." I noticed she continued to play wit her pussy. Both the shower water, and her thicker secretions ran down her juicy thighs. It was easy for me to decipher between the two.

I stepped back holding on to her waist, bent her over, and stepped behind her. I applied a small trace of the wash on my finger tip, then worked that big head into her real slowly. Natalia arched her back and moaned. "Go slow, daddy. At least at first. Don't hurt your baby. Unnnn." She moaned, stepping on her pretty toes.

I held the sides of her ass and eased my way inside nice and slow. Her hole was tight, almost suffocating. It was so hot on the inside that I almost came inside of her right away. Damn Natalia was just built for sex. The more I got accustomed to her body the more I realized that. I was glad that she was programmed like me. Glad that I would never have to worry or wonder how she felt between them legs. I had plans on fuckin this pussy and this ass for as long as it was available. After I sank as deep as I could, I remained still to allow her to get used to the feeling of me being back there.

Natalia played with her clit faster. I reached under us and helped her. "Uhhhhh, daddy. Yeah. Play wit yo baby. Ooo. I love when you touch me. I'm so obsessed wit you." She groaned, squeezing her anal walls again and again. "Fuck me. Please, daddy. Fuck meeeee-yuh."

I held that ass as I long stroked it.

Clap. Clap. Clap. Clap.

Our skins smacked into each other, louder and louder. It felt so good. With each stroke Natalia opened a bit more to accommodate my size. After the hundredth stroke she was opened just right. I was tearing that ass up with no mercy. My fingers dug into her sides. I pulled her back to me and met her with hard forward thrusts again and again while the shower rained on my back.

Natalia pushed back into me. "Yes. Yes. Fuck my ass, daddy. Fuck my ass. Uhhh shit. Daddy. Daddy. You fuckin my ass. You fuckin my ass, daddy. Un. Un. Un. Ooo. We! Yes!" She slammed back into me over and over. The scent of our fuckin rose into the air mixed with the fragrance of Ocean Breeze body wash.

Clap. Clap. Clap.

I grabbed her left breast and played with the erect nipple. I used the whole mound to pull her back to me. "Argh. Argh. Natalia. Li'l cuz. This ass. Aw shit. Aw shit cuz. Fuck. Uhhhhhhhh!" I growled, before releasing my seed deep into her. I smacked that fat ass hard, pulled out, and faced the shower. The water washed away our back door residue. I lathered my dick with the soap again and the water washed it away.

She stepped out of the tub and rubbed her box in front of me. "Come fuck me, daddy. What are you waiting on? You know you want some of this pussy. Look at it." She held the lips wide open to expose her pretty pink insides. Her clit was harder than ever. She let her middle finger draw circles around it. before she sucked the digit into her mouth.

I rushed her, picked her up, and carried her into the next room, dropping her on the bed. Without hesitating, I got between those thick yellow thighs and lined myself up.

She grabbed my waist and pulled me forward. "Fuck yo baby. Fuck me, Phoenix. Rule this pussy, daddy."

I sunk in. Her hot pussy lips wrapped around the tip, before I fell deep into that pussy. She was wet as the shower we'd just stepped out of. Her thighs spread wide open. I got in the push up position and started beating them walls like a nigga inflicting property damage. Digging in them guts. Sucking all over her neck. "Tell me this my pussy, cuz. Uhh. Fuck. Say it." More pounding. Faster and faster. "Huh. Huh. Huh. It's yours, daddy. It's yours. Aw fuck, it's yours!" She humped into me and squeezed her titties together on her chest. The long nipples peeked through the cracks of her fingers. She pulled on them and continued to enjoy the bliss of our forbidden fucking.

I pushed her titties together, and sucked on one areola after the next, pulling on them with my lips. Natalia had some pretty breasts. The nipples reminded me of pacifiers. "This my pussy, shawty. *More fucking.* Uh. This. Mine. You. Fuck! It's so good. You. *Harder pounding.* Belong. To. Daddy. Tell me."

"Uhhh. I belong to you. I belong to you. It's yours, Phoenix. It's yours." Natalia opened her mouth, and threw her head back, moaning loudly. Her legs wrapped around my waist before she came hard. Her whimpering persisted.

I forced her into a ball and continued to pound her out, until I couldn't hold back any longer. Natalia screamed, and I let loose with jerk after jerk.

At the duration she pulled me down by my neck and wrapped her thighs around me. "Phoenix. Baby. I wanna do something for you and your crew, and I don't want you to look at it as a handout either. Matter of fact just think of it as a gift because I love and appreciate you so much. How does that sound?" She licked my lips, then sucked my neck hard. Her teeth bit into me. I could hear her labored breathing on the side of it. I couldn't stop my dick from getting back hard. This woman seriously did something to me that I could not explain, nor understand.

I got on all fours over her li'l body. Even though I wasn't taking no handouts, I wasn't about to pass up any opportunities to help my crew. I knew that one of the most important tools of the game was making sure that your wolves were well fed. The minute they became hungry, and it looked like you were full that's when they'd decide to put you on the menu. And I wasn't trying to be a group of killa's main entree. "What you got for us baby? Huh?" I sucked her neck and cupped her pretty titties in my big hands.

"It's for you daddy. Just a li'l gift. That's all. I just wanna do something to make you happy, along with the other moves that I am bussing for you. Is that so wrong?" She pulled me down again. We kissed for five complete minutes. Somehow I wound up in her slippery box again. Damn this girl was getting me hooked. I had to find another bitch to split my lust between or I saw myself falling in love with Natalia, and I couldn't slip like that. She was still my people, and the murderer of Kamya, my first heart of hearts.

I sat back just enough for our lips to break the contact with each other. "Awright then baby. Show me what you taking about."

She smiled up at me. "Daddy, I swear you gon love this."

Chapter 7

There were a total of twelve land lords in Orange Mound were the majority of our people lived. The next morning me and Smoke gathered all twelve land lords together, and paid up every member in our crews rent for a year. If they had baby mothers that lived in our projects, their rent was paid for a year as well. Next came all of their utilities, and then car notes. That was followed by us taking the children shopping for the bare necessities. The gift that Natalia was talking about turned out to be a million dollars in cash. After we'd got done fucking she handed me the briefcase full of bills, and they were so crisp that could tell they were straight from a bank. They even had the amounts wrapped around them. Instead of taking the cash and using it for myself I wanted to use it on my struggling slums. The Duffle Bag Cartel was eating. We were making money hand over fist.

At the same time, we were making that money we were in a sense destroying the community in a way. Little by little majority of the adults, and even some of the older teens were getting addicted to the Rebirth. Heroin was becoming an epidemic in my ghetto, and I could honestly see how it was destroying my home front. By me being conscious of this, it made all of the money we were getting bitter sweet for me. I started to feel like I should have been doing more for my hood.

I took sixty thousand dollars and went to the Aldi's grocery store that was only a few blocks over from Orange Mound. Once we were inside of the store we had the doors locked, and the mothers of our hood were able to clean that bitch out with everything they needed food wise. After that it was to the local Walmart where another sixty thousand allowed for us to do more of the same. With the remaining eighty four bands I decided that we should throw Project party and cook out. Everybody could bring a dish, and all business would be held to a minimum while the hood celebrated itself. And that's just what we did.

The females set up thirty rows of tables and filled them with all kinds of food. Another eight tables held the refreshments. We had about twenty brothers barbequing on the grills. Everywhere you looked there seemed to be a speaker blasting music. The little kids ran around chasing one another with clean clothes, and shoes on for a change. They held either soda pops, freeze pops, or some sort of ice cream in their hands. A bunch of Project bitches caroused around with the shortest skirts and shorts imaginable, showcasing those fat asses, and thick thighs. Even the ones that pushed strollers in front of them made sure that their greatest features were on full display. I laughed at that because this was the life that I was accustomed to in the Mound. These were my people. My homeland.

The Duffle Bag Cartel was on high alert. The entire Mound was shut down. I had two vans parked with armed soldiers on each entrance and exit corner. We had big ass boulders in the middle of the street so that no car could speed past our checkpoints. If a mafucka wanted to get into the Mound on this day you was pulling over, and your shit was getting searched. If you wanted to forgo all of that then you stayed yo ass away from the deck. You couldn't enter into the Mound without running into my troops, and if anything looked fishy they had orders directly from me to chop yo ass down like a cherry tree. This was my home. My people. My hood.

It was three in the afternoon, and about two hours into the Project party, when a little dark skinned girl that had to be about Shantê's age, came up to me and pulled on my pants. I was standing next to one of the homies who was barbecuing. Two armed men stood behind me scanning the expanse of the Mound. Now that I was really feeding these niggas they were ready to kill for me like menaces. I liked that shit. I was still a little taken aback by this li'l girl being able to get this close to me without somebody blocking her path. To me that was a chink in our armor. I'd have to check that shit out.

I looked down on her. "What can I do for you li'l mama?"

"Um, excuse me, Mr. Phoenix, but is it true that you're rich? And that you're the one that helped my family get some food in our house?" She was a li'l cutie pie. The sun reflected off of her beautiful dark skin. She reminded me of a girl version of India Arie.

I knelt down and laughed. "I'm not rich yet baby, but I did help your family. Did you get enough, or what's the matter?" I asked resting my hand in her shoulder.

She shook her head. "Oh, nothing is the matter. I just wanted to say thank you. My family needed your help because my daddy is a dope fiend and we ain't have no food. I like these shoes, too. Now the kids at my school can't talk about me no more." She held up her right foot, she had on a pair of pink and black And One's, no doubt, Walmart specials. That hurt my heart.

"Say, baby, what's your name?"

"Cookie."

"Cookie? Why they call you Cookie?"

"Because it's by favorite food, duh." She rolled her eyes and laughed.

I laughed as well. "Where do you live Cookie?"

She turned around and pointed. Just across the parking lot, and a few buildings over. It's me, my mama, and my daddy."

I nodded. I was trying to figure out how I was going to help this little girl, when a pretty dark skinned sister came, and called Cookie's name.

"Cookie. Cookie. Girl, get yo butt over here and quit messing with them folks. Come on." She yelled. The sun reflected off of her shiny forehead. I looked her up and down and confirmed that she was thick as a choke sandwich with no milk.

Cookie looked up at me. "I'm sorry, Mr. Phoenix, I gotta go or I'm gon get a whipping. But before I do, can I ask you something?"

"Cookie, let's go right now!" Her mother yelled.

I held up a hand. "Ma, hold on. She'll be there in a minute." I assured. "Go ahead li'l mama."

She pointed down the block. "Do you see that building down there. You know the one with all of the green boards all over it?"

I shielded my eyes, looked and saw what she was pointing at. It was the old Boys and Girls club, and community center. It had been closed down for over two years now. "Yeah, I see it baby. What about it?"

"Can you please open it back up for the kids in Orange Mound? We don't got nowhere to go after school. There is always a bunch of shootings going on in Orange Mound. Two of my friends have already been shot this Spring. One of them died, and if they could have been inside of there they never would have." Cookie lowered her head and sighed. "Sometimes I hate living here. Look." She pulled her sleeve to the side and showed me a big dent inside of her shoulder. It was covered with scar tissue. I could tell that something tragic had happened to this baby.

"What happened there li'l mama?" I rubbed over the spot with my fingers. I imagined that she was Shantê. My throat got tight. I felt sick on the stomach.

"I got shot last summer. I lost a lot of blood. If the ambulance people didn't get me to the hospital when they did I would have died. Please, open our club for us Mr. Phoenix. I promise that when I grow up, if I get the chance to grow up, that I'll pay you back." She stood on her tippy toes and kissed my cheek, then ran off, and grabbed her mother's hand. She waved, and they disappeared into the crowd with her mother seeming to ask her a bunch of questions.

Damn, I didn't know what to do. I glanced down the street toward the Boys and Girls Club. As I thought about everything that she'd said, I knew what I had to do not only for her, but for the children in my community as a whole. Three weeks later, and after twenty thousand dollars in cash, the Boys and Girls club was back up and running, and better than before. I was going to make it my business to make sure that those kids had everything they needed at all times. I knew it couldn't fully make up for the way that me and my Cartel were destroying the hood with our narcotics, but it was a start.

***

Alicia went into labor a week after the Boys and Girls club was back up and running. She had her cousin hit my phone an hour before the bouncing baby boy came out of her womb. By the time I made it to the hospital they told me that she had already given birth. I rushed to the room, and when I got inside she was already holding him wrapped snugly in a blue blanket. Alicia looked up at me, with sweat peppered over her forehead. "It's crazy how much this li'l boy came out looking just like you." She peeled back the blanket and handed him up to me.

I was timid at first. Shaking even. I didn't know why I was nervous, but I was. I took him into my arms and held him close to my heart a I looked into his handsome, small, caramel face. He had his eyes closed tight. The hair on his head was both curly and wavy. He looked just like Shantê when she was born. I felt a chill go through me. "What's his name?" I couldn't take my eyes off of him.

"I didn't name him yet. I felt that was a job for the both of his parents, wouldn't you agree?" Alicia asked, trying her best to sit up. Glancing over at her, she looked exhausted. It looked like having my son had taken everything out of her.

"Yeah, I agree." I felt horrible for not having been in contact with Alicia. I knew she was pregnant, but even so, I'd kept my distance. What made matters worse is because I didn't even know why. I think a part of me still resented her because she was married to Mikey, even though they were separated. I didn't know what the reason was ,but now that our child was here I needed to get my shit together. "Look, I apologize, Alicia. I know I should have been there for you a lot more. I was just..."

"Phoenix, it's okay. I don't want to do that right now. It's not about us, it's about him. What is his name going to be?" She asked pulling me down so that I sat beside her.

I looked down at the face of my son. He wiggled one of his arms out of the blanket. His hand opened and closed. I placed my finger inside of the palm. He gripped it weakly at first, and then added more pressure. That made my heart skip a beat. I couldn't believe that I had my first son. I took a deep breath and exhaled loudly. "This gotta be my junior right here. I always said that when I had my first son that I was gon name him after me. So here it is. This is Phoenix Jr."

She smiled and looked him over. Pulled his blanket back just a tad. "Well, you're his father so I'll grant you that." She rubbed his cheek. Besides, he looks like a Phoenix. He looks just like his father."

I nodded, "yeah he do don't he?" We sat there silently, just listening to my son make the noises that babies make. He even smelled good. That was important to me.

"Phoenix, I don't wanna get into a huge discussion with you over the next part that comes along with me having your son. But it's crucial that we get an understanding. How are we going to raise him?" Alicia asked sitting back on the pillow.

I sighed again and rocked him just a bit in my arms. "Alicia, based off the fact that you just gave birth to my seed I love you, and I'm willing for us to get a true understanding. I wanna raise him as drama free, and as united as we possibly can. I don't know if I'm ready for a relationship on that one on one type shit. Before we discuss that you gon have to get that divorce. We can get into that later. For now, I just wanna enjoy this glorious occasion. Phoenix is here, and he comes from both of us. I got some work to do, from here on out your or my seed ain't gotta worry about nothing. I'ma cop you a house, and fill it from top to bottom, an get li'l man everything he needs. That's my word to you, Queen, and my promise to my Prince."

Before Alicia could respond there was a knock on the door. It opened and Mikey stepped into the room with two angry looking niggas behind him with mugs on their faces.

I stood up and upped my Glock out of my pants. I held my son in my left hand, and my gun in the other. I regretted the fact that I'd told my hittas to wait in the waiting room. I knew some shit was about to pop off.

Chapter 8

"Whoa. Whoa, Cowboy. Put that heater away. I mean, I know you trying to make sure yo shawty see at least more than one day in this bitch." He spat.

His hittas stepped into the room and pulled guns from their waistbands. Both were heavy set, and dark skinned. They smelled of liquor and weed smoke. I didn't want my son inhaling those scents. He was precious, and fresh to this world of pain.

"Oh my God, y'all please don't start this crap. For God sakes. There is a baby in the room." Alicia protested. She looked nervous and afraid.

Mikey waved her off. "Shut up bitch. It ain't my baby so I don't give no fuck. I just wanna see it."

"Mane let us smoke this fool, Mikey. This fuck boy killed way too many of our brothers in Black Haven. I could snuff this nigga right here and it'll be over and done with. Fuck Phoenix, Mane. I'll splash that bitch too."

I aimed my pistol right at Mikey's face. "Bitch nigga do it, and I'll stank this chump right now. Y'all better be getting the fuck from out of here, potna. Ain't shit sweet. It's Orange Mound a nothin. Fuck Black Haven."

"Phoenix please stop talking like that. Give me my baby. You just as crazy as they is." She quipped, reaching out for Phoenix Jr. with both hands.

Mikey laughed. "Phoenix, if you don't get that gun out of my face we about to have a major problem, homeboy. I already know you ain't got that killa shit in you like you fronting to have. But you see bruh nem in each side of me, they do. One word and my niggas a push yo shit back so far you gone need one of them spray on hair linings that Tory Lanez be rocking." He laughed at his own joke.

His hittas aimed all four of their guns at me, after cocking them. That made the hairs stand up on my arms. I was familiar with rolling the city with a bunch of send offs. Every major nigga needed a bunch of low life killas that would send themselves off at his command. Just one look at the dudes that stood behind Mikey and I could tell that it's exactly what these two were. They were straight, low life, send offs.

Every part of me wanted to pull my trigger. I wanted to knock Mikey's bowling ball off of his shoulders and send that bitch rolling across the floor, but the odds were against me. More importantly, the odds were against my son. I could take the bullets that they were intending to send into me, but not him. Phoenix Jr. was just a baby. A baby that I needed to protect.

I lowered the gun and handed my son to his mother. "Here you go, shawty."

"Yeah." Mikey teased. "That's a good li'l nigga right there. Live to fight another day, Phoenix. That was real smart of you." He hauled off and smacked me with so much velocity that he split my lip. I fell to one knee and bounced right back up.

"Nigga don't you ever put a gun in my face unless you planning on pulling that trigger." He snapped and pulled his gun from his waist just as a nurse entered into the room. He and his hittas dropped their guns in the nick of time. I followed suit.

The short, white lady looked from him to me, and got a worried expression on her face. "Oh my. I'll come back later. She rushed out of the room and closed the door. I detected danger almost immediately.

I stepped into his face seething. "Bitch nigga, get the fuck out of here or we about to kill each other. Go!" I crashed my forehead into his and knocked him backward. He stumbled into the door and rushed back to me. Before he was able to make the strides to get close to me there was an incessant pounding.

The door swung inward and a white armed security guard stepped into the room with his right hand over his service weapon. "There are too many visitors up here. Three of you need to disburse immediately. The local authorities have already been contacted."

Mikey dabbed at the blood that ran from his forehead. Looked at his fingers, and then over to me. He smiled and nodded his head. "Aiight, Potna. I'll be seeing you later old friend. This shit ain't over. Not for you either, bitch." He looked past my shoulder and said the last words to Alicia. She looked terrified.

"Let's move! I won't say it again." The security guard promised.

Mikey and his hittas left out of the room. All of them took the time to mug me and nod their heads. I didn't fear them niggas. I knew that as soon as I left the hospital my first order of business was going to be me crushing his entire circle. I'd waited around long enough.

"Phoenix, you should go too. You're full of drama. I don't want you coming anywhere near our son until you leave those streets alone and you get your priorities in order. I have to protect him alone until you grow up. So, go. We'll be waiting for you. I hope you know that."

The security guard frowned and stepped closer to me. "I'm sorry, but you have to go sir. She doesn't want you here." He attempted to grab my wrist.

I yanked my hand away. "Don't put yo muthafuckin' hands on me, clown. Fuck is wrong wit you?"

"Let's go, Sir."

I bumped past him and kissed my son on the forehead. "I love you, li'l man. With all of my heart. I'll be back for you. I promise." I kissed him again. "Alicia, I love you, baby. Take a day to get some rest then I'm moving you out of the city until I figure this thing out wit Mikey. I can't have nothin happening to you or our son. You hear me?" I leaned in and kissed her lips.

She accepted my affection, though timidly at first. "You better get us right, Phoenix. You owe me at least that."

***

That night me and fifteen of my killas jumped in four Old school Chevy's from the eighties and rolled around Memphis on the hunt for any nigga that even looked like he was from Black Haven. I had one of the li'l homies driving, with me in the passenger's seat, and Smoke in the back. I had a Mach Ninety on my lap, and Smoke had an Ak47 Bin Laden edition ready for action. It was one in the morning, on a hot spring day.

"Man, instead of us rolling around looking for this fool, why don't we just chop down where he lay his head, Phoenix? The longer he's able to breathe, the stronger he gets, and the more we are in jeopardy. We gotta nip this fuck nigga in the bud. Let's do that shit tonight." Smoke said with his finger on the trigger of his Kay.

I was high off of the Rebirth and wanted to kill something in a major way. I was feening to see some form of blood, and gore. I guess what I was feeling is what happened when you mixed the Rebirth with Mollies. "Aiight, we can do that. But, before we head out to that nigga's duck off, let's spin through Black Haven and spray that bitch down like Raid on roaches."

Smoke laughed, "that sound like a plan to me. Anytime I can fuck some of those niggas over, it's a good day for me. Let's roll out, we're about three minutes away from Black Haven anyway."

Before we made that move, we pulled over our whip, and let the other troops know what the word was. After everyone got an understanding, we headed off to Black Haven ready to dump some shit down.

When we pulled up to the street that led up to the Projects, I eased out of the window and sat on the sill with the Mach ninety in hand, cocked and loaded. My face was covered with a Stephen Curry mask.

Smoke sat on the back window sill. His face was covered by another Donald Trump mask. He pulled the AK47 out of the window and cocked it. "I'm ready to kill some shit, Phoenix. Whew! Dis gon be fun, Mane!"

I wasn't looking for fun. I was looking for retribution. I had to make the citizens in Black Haven pay for Mickey's sins. As long as they were rolling with, and under him I was going to make their lives a living hell. As usual, the strip leading up to the buildings were crowded. There were people all over the place, and big groups of niggas posted up, probably serving packages of that Boy. I didn't give no fuck. These dudes represented Mikey to me, and in my heart I had so much hate for Mikey that I couldn't think straight. I aimed at the first group of twenty I saw and sprayed.

Boom. Boom. Boom. Boom.

A few of them flailed before hitting the ground. My bullets chopped into their flesh back to back, and with no remorse.

Smoke followed suit. Yacking with his chopper.

Thitta-dat. Thitta-dat. Thitta-dat. Thitta-dat. Thitta-dat.

More people fell.

The rest of our troops in the cars behind us began to chop as well. Fire spit from the barrels of their fully automatic weapons. We sped up and drove all on the sidewalks chopping their shit down. I dropped one empty clip inside of the car and reloaded with another one. Without missing a beat, I cocked the Mach and was right back chopping. I literally watched about forty of so of my bullets tear into our enemies.

The goons from Black Haven bussed back, with little success. Fully automatics were the perfect toys for the perfect war we had going in with these clowns. I would make sure that Mikey become like a plague to them. As long as he was a part of their outfit, or first in command of their deck they would experience the wrath of me and my Orange Mound lunatics.

Our car hit a nasty U turn, and then stormed back in the opposite direction. We finished chopping shit down going that way. When we got half way down the block that led out of Black Haven, about fifty police appeared to come out of nowhere.

Our driver slammed on the brakes and Smoke fell off of his window sill, and into the street. I dropped my Mach and wound up holding on to the side of the car before sinking down in the seat. Smoke jumped through the window with his Kay in his hand.

"Get the fuck out of here, bruh. Hurry up, nigga, or we about to go to jail, and I ain't going. My money just starting to get right."

Our driver stepped on the gas and the car started going in reverse at top speed. He spun it around and floored it.

There was a bunch of shits being fired behind us. I was feeling sick because I had dropped my Mach. Fuck, I prayed the pigs wouldn't find it, but I already knew how shit worked. The Mach was basically a death sentence for me. The state of Tennessee was about to be all over my ass.

The police's sirens blared in hot pursuit. I could see three squad cars. The others were engaged in a shootout behind us with our troops. To be honest, I was hoping that none if our hittas back there got injured and apprehended. If they got hit, I prayed that they died before the police could get their hands on them. A dead man could tell no tales, and a corpse couldn't take the stand against you. Money didn't and couldn't make them loyal. That shit had to be in you. I feared them getting caught and spilling all of the beans. That would be fucked up.

The driver drove over a sidewalk, and down a gangway. He stormed alongside a building and wound up in the alley speeding down it like a bat out of hell. One of the squad cars was still on our ass.

"Lose that muthafucka, Homie. Punch this bitch!" Smoke ordered.

"I'm trying. I'm trying. This old ass Caprice ain't hitting like that. This ma'fucka only go a li'l past eighty. They driving Twenty Nineteens, my nigga, wit nitro fluid." He came out of the alley and made a hard right. The driver took a side street where even at two in the morning there were plenty kids out jumping double Dutch and running back and forth.

Smoke got on his knees in the back of the car. "Man, fuck this." He put the Kay on his shoulder and aimed. *Thitta-dat.* The back window shattered. *Thitta-dat. Thitta-dat. Thitta-dat. Thitta-dat. Thitta-dat. Thitta-dat.* His Kay spit, wetting the windshield of the squad car. It took three of the bullets before it exploded loudly. *Thitta-dat. Thitta-dat. Thitta-dat. Thitta-dat.*

The squad car swerved and slammed into a parked car. It caught fire right away.

"Hell yeah!" I shouted. "Take that next alley up there, and let's jump out of this bitch after you park it in a garage. We gotta split up. Them boys on our ass." I could hear more gun shots ringing off in the distance. It sounded like our troops and the law was getting it in. Man, I felt sick as a bitch.

The driver parked the car in the first open garage and cut the engine. "What the fuck we do now, bruh? They everywhere." He looked from me to Smoke in a panic stricken state.

Boom. Boom.

The bullets from my Glock knocked two chunks from the side of his head. He fell against the window of the car. Blood spattered all over it, along with his Ramen Noodles. The less witnesses we had to relive this night the better. I didn't really know the driver like that, so I didn't trust him. He had to go. It was as simple as that.

"Damn, bruh, you beat me to the punch. I was finna do the same thang. Come on, let's get the fuck out of here." Smoke said opening the back door and wiping the Kay down. He left it in the back seat, and we broke camp.

***

That night I hugged up with Natalia , while we sat on the king sized bed at the Waldorf Astoria hotel, and watched the news. The scene was reminiscent of the last time my killas had went at Black Haven, only this time there were more casualties on each side, and a few police were taken in the process. The city was guaranteed to be shut down for a few weeks at the very least. To say that I wasn't worried would have been an understatement. I had not gotten the full report of our posts. I didn't know who had been apprehended, if anybody had, and I was more paranoid than a coke head going to see his P.O.

"Damn, baby, we gotta get you out if this city for a li'l while. What do you think about taking a trip to Puerto Rico? I got a few game changers I need for you to meet anyway."

As I watched the reporter walk up and down the block of Black Haven I knew it was in my best interest to be missing in action for a minute. "Can I bring my daughter and Smoke wit me?"

Natalia squealed, and straddled me. "Oh baby, you can bring whoever you want. I'll have the jet fired up first thing in the morning."

Ghost

Chapter 9

We arrived in San Juan, Puerto Rico, at five o'clock the next day. Natalia had us booked into the W. Grand Hotel. She gave my cousins Sabrina and Shantê their own Presidential suite. Smoke had his own, and of course me and her were going to share one, even though I was trying to get out of that shit. Stepping off the jet, I'd seen one too many bad Rican bitches that looked like candy to my eyes. While I was down on the island vacationing, I wanted to sample more than a few of them. What was the use if vacationing on an island full of dime pieces if you couldn't taste their nectar? I didn't know, and I wasn't going.

After everybody was settled into their rooms, Natalia came and slipped me a black card. "Here, daddy. While you're down here all expenses are on me. I know you could foot the bill in your own, but I want you and your clan to have a special time on me. Is that okay?" She kissed the side of my neck.

"That sounds good to me baby. I'll do just that. Besides, I wanna spoil my daughter, and Sabrina. I ain't hardly spent no time wit them since, well, since Kamya passed."

She sighed and nodded. "Yeah, I know. Life had simply been so demanding. I've been neglecting a lot if things as well. I have to get back on my game, and the meetings I'm goin to set up for you while we're here are going to definitely get me back on them. Can I ask you a question ?"

I pulled my beater over my head, and stepped out on the huge balcony that over looked the ocean, and portions of the old city. Everywhere I looked there was cobble stone. The streets appeared crowded. The sun was shining brightly in the sky. It was hot and humid. The light reflected off of my abs, and chiseled chest. "What's that Natalia?"

"Sabrina is our blood cousin right?"

"Yep, what about it?"

She slid her arms around my waist and rested her face on my shoulder. "Have you and her ever had a thing before?" She kissed my neck.

I gazed out in to the street and saw a group of pretty ass Puerto Rican women. They were walking up the street in short miniskirts, and tight beaters that showcased their areolas. They were a tad slimmer than Memphis girls but not by much. I found myself curious. I wanted to know what that Spanish shit was like. And it wasn't like I hadn't had a Spanish girl before, but I'd never smashed one from their mother land, on their mother land you feel me? "Nall me and Sabrina ain't never had a thing before."

"Damn that's a pity. She so gorgeous. I would have loved to watch you two make love, and then join you. What's hotter than our family? Nothing. That's what." Her hands came up and rubbed over my chest. She breathed heavily into my neck.

I was confused. "All n'all, shawty, I got you mistaken. We've definitely fucked on kissing cousins type shit but there was never any feelings involved kind of like what me and you have for one another. Me and her were just having fun for the night. Most of her niggas been lames. Sabrina got this fat li'l clit too that keeps her pussy wet. When we were little, about eleven, and twelve years old she'd always dare me to stick my hand in her panties while she counted to a hundred, and I would. Only, she never made it that far. She'd only get to about seventy something before she was cumming all over me. It went from her cumming on my fingers, to cumming on my tongue, to cumming on my piece. She took my virginity."

Natalia shuddered against me. "I want her, Phoenix. I want all of us to fuck before we leave Puerto Rico. Just one big family. Jesus Christ, I just love our blood line so much." She turned me around and kissed my lips. Turned her head sideways and held the back of my head. Her tongue worked past my lips.

I gripped that fat ass that was encased in a red Burberry skirt. She was barefoot. Her toes were pretty as heaven. That was one thing I looked for when it came to the physical make of a woman. She had to have pretty pedicured toes, along with freshly groomed fingernails, because I was stickler for that, I made sure that I kept my shit up as much as possible. Our kissing started to get me hard. I was feening for her pussy. Was already imagining what it felt like, and how things would look with her and Sabrina both in the bed with me at one time. Sabrina was light caramel and strapped. Jazzy, and a straight freak in the bedroom. Most of the nasty shit that I'd experienced in life I'd experienced them first with her. She'd turned me out at a young age, even though she only had me by about seven months.

"Phoenix. You want some of me right now? Huh daddy? Please say yes. Tell me you wanna fuck me. I need to hear it." Natalia moaned, and slid her hand into my pants. She gripped my dick and squeezed it.

"Daddy! Daddy! Daddy!" Shanté yelled. She threw open the door to our suite and ran across the room toward the balcony.

Natalia took her hand out of my pants and turned her back to us. Her long, curly hair fell past her waist, and trailed over the humps of her ass. She was bad. I was becoming addicted to her as much as I hated to admit it.

Shantê ran and jumped into my arms and wrapped her legs around my waist. "Daddy. I can't believe we're in Puerto Rico. It's so cool. Can we go swimming soon?" She asked, looking into my eyes.

I smiled and brushed her hair out of her brown face as I kissed her soft cheek. "Of course, we can, baby. I thought you'd want to go shopping first. I guess I was wrong." I teased.

"No. No. No. We can go shopping first. I always wanna get new things. That's the best. But maybe if we don't go swimming today then we can go to the beach tomorrow? Would that be okay daddy?"

Man, his could I say no to my baby girl? She was so perfect. "Of course, baby. It's your world. You gon say hi to Natalia?"

She waved. "Hey Natalia. How are you?"

Natalia stepped over and rubbed her back. "I'm good. Thank you for asking, Shantê. I have some business to take care of, but I want you and your dad to have a great time together. Phoenix, see if you can work with Sabrina. Maybe after Shantê has the time of her life, and goes down for the night, us three can play some cards together." She smiled devilishly and kissed my cheek before disappearing into the hotel.

As soon as she was gone, Shantê frowned, and wiped her kiss off of me. "Ugh. I hate when they kiss you daddy. You're my dad. Nobody kisses my dad but me." She kissed my cheek and held my neck tightly.

Sabrina came out on to the balcony. Her hazel eyes popped in the bright sunlight. "Girl you had me worried about yo li'l butt, and here you are the whole time. Next time you better tell me when you're going somewhere. You hear me?" She chastised, frowning at Shantê.

"I was missing my daddy that's all. I'm sorry, cousin." Shantê held me tighter.

"Yeah I bet. Anyway, Phoenix. What we finna do out here? You got us all the way in Puerto Rico. I know we finna turn up, ain't we?"

I nodded. "You already know we is. First things first I'ma take y'all shopping and blow a bag on the both of you. How's that sound?"

"Like I'm finna go put my shoes on, that's how." She rushed into the hotel with her ass jiggling in her skirt. Sabrina was stupid strapped. I hadn't hit that pussy in a while, but she was definitely on my radar.

***

That evening I spent four hours in the San Juan's version of Rodeo Drive, while both Shantê and Sabrina ran in and out of the designer stores with bags on bags. Shantê acted like she wanted to buy everything in every store. Sabrina tried to be modest at first, but after I told her to go crazy, she did just that. Before it was all said and done we had so many bags that there was barely any room for us to sit inside of the stretch limousine. After a short stop at Laser Tag, followed by Pizza Playhouse, Shantê wore herself out. She was knocked out before we got back to the hotel.

Once there, I took her out of her clothes and placed her inside of a pair of Fendi pajamas before I tucked her in and kissed her forehead. When I turned around Sabrina was standing in the door way. She had her hand on her hip, and her leg cocked out. I jumped just a little bit from being caught off guard.

"Damn, you scared the fuck out of me."

"That li'l girl loves you, Phoenix. All she do is talk about you all day and all night long. You're her heart. You bet not break it either."

I kissed Shantê again and stood up. What would make you say something like that?" I made my way over to her until we were face to face.

She peered into my eyes with her hazel ones. "I'm just saying." She turned her back to me and slid her blouse over her head. She had on a red bra. Sabrina grabbed a brush off of the dresser and began brushing her silky hair.

I stepped behind her and placed my chin in the crux of her neck as I trailed my hands around her rib cage and brought them up until I was cupping her C cup titties. The material was so thin that her nipples could be made out in her the reflection in the mirror.

She leaned back into me and tried to push me away. "Move Phoenix. This ain't that type of party. The only reason I came down here is because I know I gotta keep an eye on Shantê. You have a lot going on right now. I don't want her to slip through the cracks."

I stepped forward with my front leaning into her back side. It was so soft and plump. I pulled her back into me and held her trapped there. My cheek rested against hers. "What you trying to say? I'ma get my daughter hurt or something?" I sucked hard in her neck.

She inhaled and groaned. "N'all, I'm not saying that Phoenix. I just want to look after her. That's all. That's my li'l cousin, and I love her. Her mother ain't on shit, so I gotta be on my square for her." She wiggled out of my embrace and pushed me. "Besides, I thought you was still mad at me anyway, for not telling you about Mikey hearing you and Alicia fuckin around way back when."

My eyes went straight to her breasts. Her nipples were rock hard and poking against the material of her bra I could see the dark circles as clear as day. They looked mesmerizing. "That's old news, Sabrina. We family. Family don't hold grudges against one another." I stepped back to her and pulled her forcefully to my body. We were forehead to forehead. Her eyes peered into mine. I could feel her hot breath on my lips. Her perfume was Fendi. It complimented her body chemistry and made me hunger for her. All of the things we used to do as kids came back to me, one by one. Scene after scene. Sabrina had to be one of the freakiest li'l girls in the family. She kept my hand in her panties.

"Let me go Phoenix. You making me feel some type of way. Ain't yo bitch gon get mad of she find out you're in the next room trying to smash yo cousin? Ain't she paid a lot of good money to get us down here? Got us flying on private jets and thangs. What she gon say Phoenix? Huh?"

I tilted my head, and smushed Sabrina's titties together. First, I sucked one hard nipple through the bra, and then the other one. When I got done they were both standing tall like erasers on a pencil.

Sabrina moaned, and threw her head back. "You always doing something. You can't never behave. Damn, Phoenix."

I moved her skirt up her waist and slipped my right hand into her panties. My middle finger separated her labia. She was already wet. Her big clit poked out at the top of her valley. I diddled it. This made her shake. Her nails dug into my shoulders. I pulled my finger out and sucked it into my mouth. "Mmm, you remember you used to dare me to taste your li'l kitty all the time. Remember? Our parents would be in the other room while we locked your door and did all that nasty stuff that we used to do. You remember that?"

Sabrina opened her mouth and squeezed her eyes tight. Get yo hand out of my panties Phoenix. Please. We can't do this right now." She spaced her feet.

I rubbed her peach. It was as bald as it was back then. As long as I'd known Sabrina she'd always kept that kitty nice and bare. "Tell me to touch you, Sabrina. Tell me where to put my finger."

She leaned forward and rested her lips on my neck. "Cuz, please. You gon make me relapse. I'm trying to get over our past. Please." Her feet spaced further apart.

I pulled her panties down her thighs and kept them around her knees. I felt all over that sex and kept sucking my fingers simultaneously. She tasted good. Forbidden. I leaned into her and kissed her juicy lips again. I was sure that she could taste herself, and that heightened my arousal. My tongue lashed out to lick across her bottom lip. I could feel her shiver against me. My fingers continued to play in her garden. "You want me to stop Sabrina? Huh?" Her heat wrapped around my middle finger as it slipped into her.

Her eyes closed. Her mouth opened, emitted a deep groan. Then her cheek was against mine. "Stop Phoenix. Mmmm. I don't want to relapse. We can't do this again." Sabrina pulled my hand from her panties, took a step back and lowered her skirt. Her eyes were bucked as she looked over my shoulder and cleared her throat.

I was horney as hell and confused. I turned around to see Shantê trying to sit up in the bed. She rubbed her eyes with closed fists. "Daddy, can you lay wit me until I fall back to sleep? I just had a bad dream, and now I'm scared." She said pulling back the blankets.

"I gotta take a shower. Thanks a lot Phoenix." Sabrina rolled her eyes, and brushed past me, and disappeared into the bathroom.

I took a deep breath and looked over to Shantê.

"Make room baby, cause here I come."

Ghost

Chapter 10

I don't know what kept Natalia so busy the first night we were there, but every time I hit her phone my messages went unanswered and I didn't know that she even read the first one until five o'clock the next day. By that time, me and Smoke were rolling through San Juan in a fire red, drop top Phantom, with the all-white leather seats. Since he was younger than me by about five years, he still had that stunting shit in his blood real tough, so I allowed for him to drive while I sat in the passenger's seat with twenty thousand dollars in cash in my lap. I knew it was silly as hell to have that kind of scratch laying around all willy nilly, especially with us being in a foreign land and all, but I was like fuck it. There were so many bad bitches out and about that we had to get our shine on.

Smoke leaned his seat all the way back and stuck his left elbow in the leather while he drove with his right. It had to be every bit of a hundred degrees outside, and the humidity was rough. I didn't mind cruising around in the drop top, but the sun was kicking my ass. I felt like it was melting away my wave grease. Smoke flew past the lights and slowed the whip as he came upon three Rican girls that were walking down a cobble street with big bath towels draped across their shoulders. One of them, a bit darker than the other two, and a pinch thicker, carried a picnic basket in her left hand. She rocked a pair of white shorts that hugged her ass perfectly.

I nodded over at them. "Bruh, you see dem bitches, Mane?"

"Do I see em'? Nigga that's the reason I slowed down." He pulled along the curb and cleared his throat. "Say Mamacitas, what it do boo boo?"

They looked over at us and smiled. I noticed the darker one glanced in my direction but kept right on her merry way as if she wasn't interested at all. That intrigued me. It presented a challenge, and I was all for that.

Smoke tapped the expensive horn and threw his arms up. "What, we can't get no play? Shawty y'all don't jam wit country boys a something?"

One of them giggled. She had short, curly hair, and rocked a pair of tan booty shorts, and a tank top. I could see her bikini underneath it. She pointed toward the beach. "That's where we're headed." She said in a heavy accent. "We'll meet you over there." Her pack had left her a bit behind. She jogged and caught up with them. Her ass jiggled. Her shorts became lost inside of her crack, revealing more of the golden globes.

Smoke shook his head. "Damn these hoes bad down here bruh. What you wanna bet that I get at least two of them to come to my bed tonight. I don't give a fuck of they sisters." He made his way down to the huge beach, that was filled with white sand.

The street that we were on led directly to the beach anyway. It kind of spooked me because everywhere I looked there appeared to be nothing but blue water. The ocean was huge. That freaked me out a li'l bit. I started to imagine shit about hurricanes, and the island being swallowed by water before we could get back on the jet. I had never learned to swim, and with all of this water surrounding their city it had my anxiety on high. But the sight I saw when we arrived at the beach had me in awe. It was flooded with bad bitches.

Smoke parked the whip but kept a track by Yo Gotti banging out of the speakers. "Yeah nigga, I'ma brang a li'l bit of Memphis down here." He nodded his head and sat on the hood of the Phantom.

I shielded my eyes from the sun, before grabbing my pair of gold framed Cartier's from the car. Once I slipped them boys on I was good to go. I was on the search for the darker Rican with the picnic basket. Once I located her, I was off in her direction. "Bruh I'ma fuck wit you in a minute. I need to see what's good with the one that was carrying the picnic basket."

Smoke smiled, his gold teeth shined in the sunlight. "Shawty was thick as hell. You gon head, Mane. I'ma see what it do wit these two that's making their way over to me right now. They definitely look related." He dusted off his clothes and grabbed a box of Garcia Vegas off if the back seat that were already rolled up with some of that good Memphis Loud.

As I walked past the two Ricans, one of them grabbed my wrist. "Ay Papi, where do you think you're going?" She asked, looking me up and down. She had dark brown eyes, that fit her pretty oval face.

I laughed. "Aw shawty, my li'l brother got a bug he wanna put in y'all ear. Me personally I'm digging shawty right over there." I nodded toward the third female that had been a part of their party. I saw her setting up an area on the sand. There was a gentle breeze that coursed through.

"Melania?" She asked. "What's the matter with us?"

"Yeah, what's the matter with us?" Her mate chimed in.

"Nothing, I guess I'm just a fan of the chase." I continued on my path. Before I got too far, I glanced over my shoulder one time to see Smoke sliding his arms across their shoulders. He'd already lit a few blunts and was handing them one a piece.

The sand crunched under my Jordans as I made my way across it in hot pursuit of Melania. When I got to where she was setting up her things, she was on all fours spreading the towels out side by side one another. I stood there for a second, casting a shadow over her.

She shielded her eyes from the sun and looked up to me. "Uh, can I help you?"

"You most certainly can." I knelt a bit and extended my hand. "My name is Phoenix. I'ma a Memphis boy, and it's a pleasure to meet you shawty."

She looked me up and down. "I don't know you, and I don't mess with boys of any sort. Far as that shawty stuff, that's not my name. And if that's the best rap that you have, you'll never learn my name. Now if you will get going I need to tan." She took a bottle of sunscreen from her small bag that I'd missed, and squirted a nice portion into her hand, before rubbing it into her arms.

I stood there perplexed. No, this li'l bitch didn't just shit on me like that. Not only was I shocked, but I was even more attracted to her. I see she was about to make me put up a fight. I knelt down on both knees. "I apologize, let me start again. My name is Phoenix. I'm from Memphis, Tennessee. This is my first time out of the country and it's a pleasure to be on your island."

Melania continued to rub the sunscreen into her skin in various places. Her complexion was gorgeous, almost a honey color. She smelled as sweet as sin and looked even better to me. Her short, curly hair blew in the wind. Her eyes were light brown, with neatly arched eye brows. Her nails and toes were French tipped. She exuded high maintenance. I liked that. "Well Phoenix. I hope you enjoy yourself on the island. It's a beautiful place to be. There is a lot to do down here, and a lot to see." She pulled her shorts off tossed them to the side and laid out flat on her stomach.

My eyes went right to her rounded ass. Honey colored like her skin, it got darker towards the top of her thighs. It looked good. Real good. "I'm saying Melania. What would it take to get you to show me around this bad boy?"

"I'm not a chauffeur, nor am I a call girl. I'm pretty sure you could Google either one of those services though. They shouldn't be hard to find. Have a good day though. I wish you the best." She turned around to look up at me. "You're blocking my sunlight.

I took a step to the side. She laid her face on her hands and closed her eyes. I felt angry and irritated. It had been a while since I'd tried to holler at a female and this one was giving me the cold shoulder. I felt like she was knocking a major chunk out of my self-esteem. I hadn't been here in a long time.

Smoke came over with his arms draped over both women. He kissed the cheek of one, and then the other. "Man, this sun hitting like a ma'fucka, Phoenix. I ain't tryna get all sweaty and shit so we just gon chill for a few and den I'ma take shawty 'nem to the Telly and show em' what that Presidential suites shit look like. They say they ain't never been in one before." He looked from one girl to the next, and then down to Melania. His eyes bugged out of his head when he saw the humps on her lower back.

"Smoke let's go over to the juice stand and get something to drink. You can tell us more about this Memphis thing." One of the Puerto Rican girls said, with her arm around his waist.

He smiled. "That sounds like a plan to me. Fuck wit you in a minute Potna." They turned and walked away.

Smoke hand his hands on each of their asses, rubbing all over them.

"Ain't you going wit 'em?" Melania asked, with her eyes still closed. She moved in the slightest and her cheeks jiggled. Her thick thighs looked both solid, and soft. I wanted to take a bite out if one of them. I had to have her. One way or the other.

I pulled my Ralph Lauren over my head and dropped the shirt in the sand. Next came my white beater. There were two towels that were folded up beside her. I took one of them and laid it out flat.

She looked over at me. "That is my sister's towel, what are you doing?"

I situated myself before I grabbed her bottle of sun screen and started rubbing it all over my chest and abs. "You see, I don't know how they get down out here in Puerto Rico shawty, but I'm from the Durty South, and down there we go for what we want and don't give up easily."

I squirted some more of the product into my hand and rubbed it all over my arms and shoulders. "Now I like what I see. I can tell there is something different about you. You're beautiful, and jazzy. Clearly you don't know who I am, but we'll work on that later." I handed her the bottle and turned away from her.

"What's this for?"

"For you to put it on my back. I noticed you got the majority of your body, and you missed your whole back. After this sun gets done baking yo ass you gon look real weird. So... Come on. My back please."

She knelt holding the bottle for a moment, then I heard the top pop off of it. "You're lucky I'm a courteous person.

Or else I'd let you fry." When her small, soft hands began gliding all over my back I felt like I was in heaven.

"I appreciate this Melania."

"Who told you my name? Was it one of my annoying big sisters?"

I shrugged my shoulders. "Maybe it was God himself."

She smacked her lips. "I seriously doubt that. But whatever." Her hands continued to glide all over my back. "What's your deal anyway?"

"My deal is that I wanna take you out to dinner tonight so I can get to know you. When was the last time a man spoiled you? Or treated you like a queen?"

She scoffed. "I don't need a man to treat me like anything. If I want to be spoiled, I'll spoil me. If I want to go out to dinner I'll take myself out. I get my own money. I'm my own Queen. I define me. You understand that?"

I did. "Well yet and still, I would love to have the opportunity to get to know you better. Something about you is alluring to me."

She finished with my back and dropped the bottle on the last towel that hadn't been unfolded as of yet. "There you go. You're welcome."

"Thank you. And?"

"And what?"

"So, you're going to allow me take you out or what?"

"No, I'll pass. I don't know you and you probably aren't going to be here long enough for me to get to know you. It's a pure waste of time. Life is too short. But thank you for your multiple compliments." She turned back on to her stomach, and closed her eyes, laying her head in her arms.

Smoke walked back over with the two sisters. They set up beside Melania, and he knelt beside me, and leaned into my ear. "Bruh these li'l bitches trying to get smashed. They tryna fuck wit both of us. I wanna see how fucked up we can get 'em, and then watch them eat each other's pussy before we smash 'em. You know, bring that Memphis shit to Puerto Rico. What you think?"

I watched both broads stand up and wiggle out of their tiny shorts. Their fat asses bounced as it left the confines of the shorts. They were only a tad bit slimmer than Melania. They looked so much alike that they resembled twins. I could definitely watch them get down with each other with no hesitation.

"Yeah bruh, I'd like to see that shit too." I looked down at Melania and wished that she could have been a part of the equation. She was so fuckin bad and stuck up. I needed that in my life. But clearly she wasn't fuckin wit a nigga. So, I sighed in defeat, and eyed her sisters. "Let's make that happen."

Smoke nodded. "Say no mo', Playboy, watch me work dis magic."

Chapter 11

I sat back beside Smoke with a bottle of Moët in my hand. I was high as a bird in the sky. I had a gram of the Rebirth in my system, and two Mollies. I felt like I was floating on air.

Smoke tooted a line of the Rebirth and pulled on his nose. He took the bottle of Patron and turned it up. Guzzling like a fish thirsty for water. On the table was twenty thousand dollars in ones and tens. The whole top of it was covered. The girls had promised to put on a strip show for us that we wouldn't forget. I was looking to hold them to that.

"Say bruh, I still don't know which one of these bitches is which." I admitted.

Smoke's eyes were lower then a midget's ankles. "Mane it's simple. You see Cee Cee got the short curly hair, and Monni's hair is a li'l longer. Cee Cee is older by a year. You got it now?"

I nodded. "Yeah, I got it." I nodded my head to Cardi B's 'Money' track that played in the background.

The door to the bathroom cracked open. Cee Cee stuck her head out. "Y'all ready for us?" She asked with her lips painted a cherry red.

Smoke jumped up and dimmed the lights. "Hell, yeah." He pointed the remote control at the sound system and turned it up some more. "Let's go, shawties. Welcome us to Puerto Rico the right way." He took his seat beside me and grabbed a stack of money.

I did the same. I was ready to fuck one of these bitches. I didn't care which one it was. "Let's get this bitch cracking. Natalia has been blowing my phone up. I'm ghosting her ass just like she did me."

Smoke laughed.

Cee Cee stepped out of the bathroom in a short, cherry red see through robe that stopped at her hips. Underneath I could see a hint of her panties. The lace material cuffed her pussy mound and formed a prominent camel's toe. Her thick thighs appeared to be oiled up in such a way that made them glisten in the dim light. Her body gyrated to the sounds of the music. She wiggled from side to side like a snake then dropped down on all fours and popped her ass in such a way that it made the robe travel upward on to her lower back. Her cheeks displayed themselves. The panties separated the mounds in a lovely fashion.

Monni stepped out next. She rocked a purple, see through robe that clung to her curves. She opened it, to reveal a one piece body suit that was split up top so that her D cup breasts nearly spilled out of them. Her nipples poked against the fabric. She dropped down to her knees and, crawled across the floor slowly. Monni got beside her sister and popped her ass just as much. Almost in unison, they turned around so that their asses faced us. Both ladies spread their knees and twerked hard on beat.

I jumped up and grabbed a stack of money, stood over them and made it rain. I fanned bill after bill over their twerking bodies. These li'l bitches was bad.

Smoke took two bundles of cash and threw them in the air. The bills slowly traveled from the ceiling and spilled all around us. He started rubbing all over Cee Cee's ass. Then he yanked her panties to the side and exposed her naked pussy lips. Smoke pressed his face against her back side, eating her out from the back.

Cee Cee arched her back, and moaned as she grabbed at the carpet, and spread her knees further apart. She even reached under herself and yanked her panties all the way to the side to assist smoke. "Ay Papi. Yes. Ooo, fuck yes."

Monni stood up and stepped into my face. "You looking to give us a chance?" She asked, rubbing her hand over my front. She cupped my dick through by shorts.

I pulled her to me and grabbed her ass and played with those hefty cheeks back there. She had more ass than I thought she did. It felt like it had a li'l weight to it. "Yeah, shawty. You gon put this Rican pussy on a nigga a what?"

Smoke stood up and got behind her. His shorts were open, his dick out. He rubbed the length of himself up and down her crease and pulled on her hair. "Bitch, I'm finna fuck you and your sister. Then I'ma watch y'all fuck each other. We gon brang some of that Memphis swag to the island."

Cee Cee stepped into my face and tried to kiss me on my lips. I moved my face so that they wound up on my neck. She took the hint and began sucking all over it. "Papi. I want some of this Peeto." Her hand slid past the waistband of my shorts. She grabbed my meat and groaned.

I pushed her down by the head. Unzipped my jeans and put my dick on her lips. "Come on mami. Show me what that be like."

She opened mouth wide and sucked me into it. Her hand gripped my piece, stroking it while she sucked with her jaws hollowing in and out. Then she popped it back out, and licked up and down it, coating it with plenty of spit. She sucked it back into her mouth.

I knelt down and continued to feed it to her. Grabbed another bundle of cash off of the table and threw it against her back so that it went everywhere. Cee Cee moaned around my dick and kept on sucking like a champion.

Smoke took Monni's hand and placed it on her sister's ass. "Play wit that pussy Monni. You see how juicy that ma'fucka is?"

She pulled her hand back. "No, I can't do that."

Smoke covered her lips with his own. They tongued each other for a full two minutes it seemed, all the while his hand played between her thighs. He gave her a pill.

She swallowed it and kept right on kissing him. His fingering became faster and deeper. "Uh. Uh. Uh. Papi."

He licked her neck. "Touch that pussy, baby. It's okay." He guided her hand, until it was cupping Cee Cee's pussy. Her fingers played over the lips. Then she was fingering her.

Cee Cee moaned around my dick again. "Mmm. Mmm. Mmm. Mmm."

Monni, leaned between her spread knees and before we knew it, she was eating Cee Cee hungrily. Whatever Smoke had given her seemed to work in record time.

Cee Cee pulled my piece out of her mouth and looked back at Monni. Her eyes were low. "Un. Un. Un. What are you doing? Un. Shit." She laid her face on the carpet. Her tongue ran all over her lips.

Smoke got behind, Monni, and slid into her from behind. He took a hold of her waist and began fucking her fast and hard.

She made a loud smacking sound behind Cee Cee's ass. Tilted her face to the ceiling and moaned loudly. A steady smacking sound emitted from behind her.

Cee Cee's finger's slipped between her thighs, and into her pussy. She pulled in her sex lips, brought her fingers out and sucked them into her mouth. Then she was back in her gap diddling furiously. The room quickly filled with the scent of pussy and perfume. The audio was moaning and groaning from Smoke and both sisters.

My dick jumped up and down in an excited state. I rubbed it across Cee Cee's lips again. She took a hold of it, but as soon as she did, Monni's face was back in her crotch. Something in me told me that this wasn't the first time they'd gotten down together. Cee Cee, turned around, and laid on her back. She opened her thighs wide and scooted under Monni and forced her face into her gap while she rode it from the floor.

Smoke grunted and slammed harder into Monni from behind. A thick vein appeared in the middle of his forehead. He yanked on her curly hair and pulled her head backward pounding her like a savage.

I lay on my side and fed my dick back to Cee Cee. She sucked it happily while stroking it up and down in her fist. Her head moved back and forth in rapid fashion. She whimpered around it. Popped it out and screamed. "Uhhhhh! Uhhhhhhhh! Monni! Shiiiiiittttttbitch!" She started to shake like crazy, before her thighs wrapped around Monni's head.

I waited until Cee Cee was shaking as if she were freezing cold. Then I pulled her from under Monni and flipped her on her stomach. Took a condom out of my pocket and slid it over my piece, before I entered her channel. Her tightness surrounded me. It sucked me in like a hungry vacuum. She was dripping wet.

"Aw. Aw. Aw. Papi. Papi. Ooo-a fuck me. Fuck me, Papi." She pushed backward into my lap.

"Shit! I'm cumin shawty! I'm cumming in this Puerto Rican pussy! Arrrggh!" Smoke hollered and came deep within Monni's womb, jerking time and time again.

I slapped Cee Cee's big ass hard and kept stroking. I watched my dick slide in and out of her. She was leaking like a Puerto Rican. No pun intended. My piece was making a slouching sound as it traveled in and out of her. Her golden lips were spread around my ramming penis. Juices ran down my balls and dripped off of them. It felt amazing.

"I'm cumming Papi. I'm cumming! Awwww, yes! Yes!" She laid her forehead in the carpet, pushed backward into my lap as hard as she could, before cumming all over me. I could feel her womb clenching and unclenching my piece. Milking me.

I shuddered and fucked her harder.

Monni knelt on the side of me and fingered her own pussy. "Damn. You're killing my sister." She rubbed all over Cee Cee's ass. Her fingers traveled to her kitty. "Look at how you're stretching her open." She lowered her face, and licked all over Cee Cee's sex lips, and my piece as well. Her pink tongue darted out at our coupling. All the while her hand stayed between her own legs. Her fingers were three knuckles deep inside of herself.

The sight of her eating Cee Cee, and her fingers being embedded within her dripping cat became too much for me. I couldn't take it any longer. I sped up the pace and growled.

Monni and Cee Cee started to make out. Cee Cee's hand went between Monni's thighs, her fingers entered inside of her. They darted in and out at full speed. Ooze dripped down her wrist. She bent all the way over, and I saw the gates to her pussy open up. That was it.

I came hard. Ramming into her from behind. I pulled out, and yanked my rubber off, and bussed all over her round ass, and booty crack. I was breathing harder than a fat man running after a city bus.

Monni pulled my dick out and sucked it into her mouth. She pumped it in and forced the nut to come out of me. With every stroke I felt my toes curling. I closed my eyes and laid back on the floor as I allowed for her to boss me up. Cee Cee joined in to help her. Occasionally they would stop to make out with each other, furthering my suspicion that this wasn't the first time the pair had gotten down with one another. I wondered if Melania got down as they did. She didn't seem like it, but then again looks could be deceiving. Behind closed doors everything was a different story.

"Aw shit, Phoenix it's a hit, bruh." Smoke hollered.

I opened my eyes in time to see three half masked gun men with curly hair rushing over to me and the girls. They brandished their handguns and pointed them in both me and Smoke's face.

The girls grabbed their clothes off of the floor and rushed out of the room. Cee Cee took one chance to stop and look back at me. She laughed and shook her head.

A heavy set, what I assumed to be Puerto Rican, picked me up and slammed me against the wall. "I hope you enjoyed your main entrees, and now for dessert. This is a robbery. We'll take every penny you got in this room. You got a problem with that, my nigga?" He said this sarcastically and pointed his gun under my chin. I noted that the hammer was already cocked back on it.

I already knew how to play these clowns. Usually when it came to robbers, if you made it seem that what they saw was all you had they more than likely would cut you a break. Shit usually ended there. I decided to play those cards. "Say Mane, we emptied out our accounts. This is all of the money we had to party in San Juan. Please don't do this."

He smacked me with the pistol and knocked me to the floor. "It's already been done." He said something to his goons in Spanish.

They pulled garbage bags out of their drawers and filled them with money. They even took the time to drop our liquor, Cartier glasses and blunts inside of the bags.

Smoke kept his back against the wall fuming. "Y'all just take that shit and get the fuck out of here. We were slipping. It is what it is."

One of the goons, mugged him, and pointed. He began speaking Spanish to the head goon. He drug his finger across his upper row of teeth and pointed back at Smoke.

The head goon extended his gun at Smoke. "Open your mouth Mr. Gold teeth, millionaire man."

Smoke curled his lip. "Fuck you. I ain't opening shit."

The head goon shrugged his shoulders. Boom. His bullet smacked into Smoke's shoulder, knocking a hole through it. Smoke fell to the ground, and he straddled him, beating him in the mouth with the gun again and again, cursing in Spanish.

The other two kept their guns trained on me. I felt helpless and angry. I wanted to torture these bitch niggas. Them hoes had set us up. I was sure of that. If I had to, we would search the whole island of Puerto Rico until we found them. I watched the goon pick Smoke's teeth up one by one and toss them into the plastic bag of one of his henchmen. He kicked Smoke in the ribs before they ran out of the room.

As soon as they disappeared, I rushed over to his side and knelt down beside him. He was knocked out cold, breathing ragged. His mouth was filled with blood. It oozed along the side of his face, and into his ear canal. Damn, they'd fucked my nigga up. I ran out of the room to get help.

Chapter 12
A week later...

Jacob the Jeweler spun Smoke's chair around with a smile on his face. Anybody that was somebody fucked with Jacob the Jeweler because he was known for getting mafuckas right when it came to that jewelry shit, hence his name.

Smoke grabbed the mirror and cheesed at his teeth. His entire grill was gold, but with clear diamonds all over them that looked like ice cubes. The light from the private et reflected off of his teeth and caused them to twinkle and glisten. He ran his tongue across them. Her held the mirror with his right hand. His left arm was in a sling. "Now dis what I'm talking bout here, Playboy. Mafuckas thought they did something not knowing that I was a plugged thug. You got me right Phoenix." He nodded his head and looked his grill over.

It wasn't me that had gotten him right. I was still using Natalia's black card. She had also been the one to fly Jacob the Jeweler out for him to get Smoke right. I was still feeling like shit because my nigga had got hit up, and we still hadn't gotten the opportunity of running into them clowns as of yet. Man, I couldn't wait. We had half the Cartel in San Juan now on the sole mission of hunting them punks down. "Man, you know I gotta keep you right li'l homie. Don't even worry either, we gon figure out that other situation too. You got my word on that."

He waved me off. "Don't keep tripping on that, Mane. We know what we gotta do, and more importantly I know what you would have done had we not got caught like we did. You certified in my eyes, big Homie. That's for damn sure." He looked in the mirror again. "Them hoes finna be all over a nigga dick like foreskin."

***

That night, as me and Natalia sat parked in her drop top Bentley, she reached and took a hold of my hand. We were in a huge mountain of a hill. The car was parked and directed so that it over looked the Ocean, and the entire city of San Juan. There appeared to be a million stars in the sky. "Phoenix, do you have any idea how much I love you?" She asked. Beyoncé's 'Flaws and All', played out of the speakers.

"I love you too, Natalia."

She shook her head. "No, you don't understand what I mean. I mean I love you with all of my heart, mind, body, and soul. I wish that we could be together in the natural sense. Like I really really want you to be my husband. I mean that."

I pulled a blunt out of the ashtray and sparked it. The smoke blew out of the window. It drifted upward along and covered about a million lightning bugs. "Natalia, you just in love with that forbidden shit that we do. You got that corrupt family shit in your genes just like me and you're getting your lust entangled with love. I ain't did shit for you to love me, li'l cuz. Nothin more than fuck that pussy the right way. That's it." I took a long pull from the blunt again, and inhaled deeply, blowing the smoke back out through my nose.

She let my fingers go and crossed her arms. "Damn."

I looked her over. "Damn, what Natalia?"

She shook her head. "You got me all fucked up. I can't believe that you would even think the way that you do. Let me tell you something, Phoenix. Before you came into my life, it was filled with hell. Ever since I was a little girl the family on by mother's side treated me like shit simply because I had Black inside of me. They called me names. Made me eat at family functions all alone. Beat me anytime I did anything wrong, and here's the kicker, as much as the men in my family degraded me for being mixed, and all of that stuff, it never stopped them from taking advantage of me every chance they got. My mom knew what they were doing, and she said nothing. Not a fuckin word. In fact, there was a time when she walked in on her uncle doing some shitty things to me, and she simply excused herself and left f the room again. He proceeded to screw me all that night. I was barely fourteen. I grew to hate the Russian side of my family. I hated my mother. She never protected me. She never even acted as if she loved me until you came into the picture. You reminded her of my dad. You made her see him inside of me again, but by that time it was much too late. I'd already planned her murder in my head, and I knew it would be by my own hands. It was long overdue."

She stared off into the distance. Her eyes were bucked and unseeing. "Phoenix, throughout the years I became obsessed with finding my father's family. I yearned to have a piece of him. A piece that I had never known. Then you came, and you look so much like his pictures. You're like a representation of him. I need you in my life, and I love you. You're my only connection to the family and bloodline I was deprived of having. The only physical link to my dad. That's one of my main reasons for loving you in the way that I do. I feel that we belong together and that only you can help to heal me. You are you, but you are also my dad. Know it sounds weird, but hopefully you get it."

I had my head lowered. I didn't know what to say to all of that. That was most definitely a lot to take in. But I had to look at things logically. Natalia was a link to so many openings in the game for me. She had vast wealth, and political connections due to her Russian side of the family. Connections that I knew I would need one day soon. Aside from that, I cared about her. She was beautiful, vulnerable, and appeared to be crazy about me. Yeah it might have been a taboo kind of crazy, but what else was new? I was down to roll with her. She'd grown on me heavily, and from the looks of things, it appeared that we were all that we had. As much as I hated to admit it, I needed her. There weren't too many females in the hood flying private jets, dudes either, in fact the only niggas in the hood that I knew flying on jets were me, and Smoke, and that was courtesy of Natalia. So I'd've been crazy to let Natalia go no matter how I looked at the situation .

I reached into her lap, and took her hand, and interlocked our fingers. I had to play my role. My future as well as my daughter's depended on it. "Baby, I love you despite our relation." I exhaled and paused for dramatic effect. "I'm sorry that you had to go through all of the things that you have. I wish you would have told me that when we were in Moscow, I swear I would of went on a rampage over you." I pulled her head to my shoulder and kissed her forehead. "We're all we got right now, Natalia. Just you, me, and Shantê. I can't stand to lose you, and I need your love baby. I need your love so so much, I swear I do. Come mere." I pulled her over, and into my lap until she was straddling me. Once Natalia was there I moved her silky curls away from her face so I could see it clearly. She was gorgeous. Even in the darkness, her blue eyes were piercing.

"Phoenix, you know that I would do anything for you. I will take you any place you wanna go. All I ask is that you love me in return. That you worship me as your woman, despite our blood. There is no woman out here that will do the things for you that I will. I will put my life on that." She brushed my cheek with the back of her hand. "You are so damn fine to me. From the first day I saw you I knew that I was crazily attracted to you. Your physical, and your scent is intoxicating. It drives me nuts. When you're in my sight I can't think straight. When you're away from me, it's even worse. My every thought is you, and the things you do, or the last things that you've either said or done to me. I worship you baby. I worship everything about you, and I feel that you could be so much more. More than the dope game. More than an average gansta in the ghetto. More than a Black man. With your drive and ambition, you could be something great. I am willing to invest some real money into you, Phoenix. Money that transcends the hood. We could conquer the real estate industry, not just here in America but abroad. We could get into Tech. Become multi-millionaires and billionaires before we're thirty-five. All it would take is for you yo go to school for a few years. You pick the college, I'll foot the bill. I believe in you Phoenix. Life is more than the slums. Can't see you that?"

I could, but I couldn't at the same time. All I knew was Orange Mound. Memphis. Trapping and pulling kick downs. Popping that iron. It was hard for me to see the things that she was getting at even though I wanted to so badly. I didn't want to be in the hood forever. I didn't like looking over my shoulder at every turn. Didn't like the feeling of being paranoid, worrying about what the law was going to do, or when that pussy nigga, Mikey was going to make his move. After a while that would drive anybody crazy. The Bible said when you lived by the sword you died by the sword. I'd been living by the sword ever since I was twelve years old. I knew it was only a matter of time before I died by it if I didn't switch up my game plan. I was simply stuck. But I had to keep Shantê at the forefront of my mind.

"Baby, I want something different. I swear I do, but I don't know the first thing about getting it. I'm just being completely honest with you. But, you know what? I'm willing to follow if you're ready to lead me to a better path that would render a better future. I think that you have my best interest at heart. So, I'm willing to try for you, and me." I brushed her lips with my own, ready to tongue her li'l fine ass down.

She turned her head away and sighed. "There is two things that I need to tell you, and I don't think you're going to be happy with either, but we have to get through it. Together. Okay?"

I frowned. "What's up?" I could sense from her body language that something was most certainly wrong.

Natalia sighed and shook her head. "Look I don't know what you and your crew did before you guys left Memphis, but the state of Tennessee has issued a warrant for your arrest on the suspicion that you were involved in the mass slaying that took place in Black Haven a few weeks back. Your picture has been all over Facebook, along with Smoke's. They're also saying that there was a gun recovered that had your DNA on it. I don't know how true any of this is, but I'm concerned for your safety. Lets just leave the country, and never come back. At least until things die down. Please."

I removed her from my lap, and went in to Facebook. Almost every social media news sight had both me and Smoke's picture plastered across it. They were calling us cold blooded killers. Saying we were the leaders of a deadly gang that called themselves the Duffle Bag Cartel.

They had five detailed pages of our so called history and make up. A reward in the amount of fifty thousand dollars was being issued for our arrest, or information leading up to our arrest. There was even an article stating that the Governor of Tennessee was looking to get the Feds to approve an indictment for terrorism. That spooked me. If that happened, I knew the Feds would spare no resources to arrest both me and Smoke. The local authorities had already arrested fifteen known Duffel Bag Cartel members. Apparently the Orange Mound had been run through by the authorities and been turned upside down. I lowered my phone and mugged her. "How long have you known about this?"

"Three days. I tried to give you some time to scroll upon it yourself, but you never did. I mean, baby, it's all over social media."

I nodded. She was right. I hadn't been on my phone in the least bit since I'd been in Puerto Rico. The last time I'd checked in the Mound was when we'd scooped a bunch of our soldiers. I was surprised that none of them came to me about this. I sent Smoke a text asking if he knew about the situation back home.

His response: Yeah, that's old news. I'ma holler at you about it tonight. Told the fellas to keep quiet until you discovered it yourself. Who told you?"

I ain't respond. I was so fuckin frustrated. "That's one thing. You said you had two. What's the other thing Natalia? You might as well get all of this shit out."

"The powers in Moscow that were loyal to my mother and grandfather have issued a bounty for my head. They want me dead and I am sure that they've hired a series of professional hitmen to do the job. And it's not just me they want though, it is also you and Mikey. They're saying that I used you two to carry out my mother's murder, and to knock off a few of her associates, when in actuality she used you two to knock off her own people, and I took her out. It's turmoil right now. The only good news is that I have a substantial amount of money in a number of off shore accounts. Money that no ones knows about other than myself. If we get a head start, we should be able to flee this country for good and disappear. I don't know what to do Phoenix, all I know is that I don't want to lose you." She tried to take a hold of my hand again.

I opened the door to the Bentley, stepped out and ran my hands over my face. Damn, that was a lot to take in at once. I felt like the world was coming down on me at full speed. I didn't have the time to brace myself. *What the fuck was I going to do*? I wondered.

Natalia eased herself out of the car. "What are you thinking, baby?"

My mind was spinning so fast that I didn't know what I was thinking. That was a lot of heat coming from all areas. I mean, it should've been expected, but it wasn't. I'd never been in this position before. "Ain't no way that nigga, Mikey, gon get away with what he did to my daughter or me. Just like I ain't leaving Puerto Rico until we find them chumps that did this shit to Smoke. Toya gotta go too. All of this is unfinished bidness that I can't let roll off of my shoulders."

"So, what do you wanna do? I'm riding with you regardless."

She stepped behind me and rested her hand on my right shoulder. "Did you hear me Phoenix?"

"Yeah. First things first, help me find these Rican dudes that knocked the homie grill out, and then I gotta touch bases with Mikey before we move off into the next

108

stage of life. My heart a never be able to accept what he did to Shantê. That's just that."

Natalia nodded. "Okay, I got you. We're in this together, right?" She came around and took my face into her small hands. Her blue eyes searched my own in the moon light.

I felt so disconnected from her. It felt like I was mentally and emotionally grained. I felt trapped, like I was against the ropes, and being beaten time and time again by a heavyweight boxer called Life. I'd never felt so defeated. Now wasn't the time to wear my heart on my sleeve. I just couldn't. I looked back into her eyes. "Yeah baby, it's just me and you. Against all odds, and until the death."

"That's all I needed to hear." She wrapped her arms around my neck, stepped forward, and kissed my lips. "Let's turn up."

Ghost

Chapter 13

"Mane, what type of shit are we rolling into? This look like a third world country, bruh." Smoke said this with two automatic Forty Fives on his lap, ready for action.

I continued to roll down the dirt road that had metal shacks in each side of it. There appeared to be hundreds of them. The road was so narrow that part of the truck was rolling over the grass of each shack as I drove down it. It was two in the morning, and hot as hell. This shit was so humid that it felt like a plastic bag was being held over my head, before we got into the truck and cranked the air conditioner. "Shawty say they call this bitch, Death Alley. This is San Juan's version of the Orange Mound. The poorest of the poor live here, and the lowest of the low. We gotta be on our P's and Q's. At the same time, we on our Duffle Bag shit. Since we already got the laws and every other ma'fucka barreling down on us, we gon make whatever time they trying to give us worth it, besides, you my right hand Smoke. These pussy niggas gotta pay for what they did to you. It's as simple as that."

Smoke continued to look out the window. There were about five scantily clad females pacing back and forth. As we rolled past they waved at the truck and tried to get us to stop so we could sample their sexual delights. One even had the nerve to raise her shirt and show off her supple breasts. She squeezed them together solicitously. "You know what Phoenix, that's why I fuck wit you, homeboy. Ever since I came under you, you've made sure that me, my family, and every nigga I put in front of you was well taken care of and eating." He wiped his nose. "If you think it's best we run through this bitch, then that's what it is." Smoke ran his tongue across his new grill. "Ain't no way I was going back home without seeking retribution for this." He looked over to me. "What's the name of this fool that we looking for?"

"Vinny. He the one that knocked yo shit out on that tough man bull crap. We gon fuck over his entire regime, though. Shawty gave me the low down on these niggas. They scum, bruh. Straight up. And that's why we got this guide in the back seat." I looked into my rear view mirror and gave the heavy set Puerto Rican woman a once over. The truck felt like it was rolling over a bunch of rocks, and gravel.

"Man, I was wondering why we had a bitch in the truck. I was gon ask you that, but I respect your leadership so much that I just knew it had to be a reason."

"It is. Apparently, these ma'fuckas done bodied both of her sons. She wants revenge, but everybody in their village is afraid to go up against these studs. But, not us, bruh. Ma'fuckas gone right the wrongs they caused us." I said curling my lip.

"In such a way." Smoke agreed.

The woman in the back seat pointed down the road. "Jew see right down dare? Wear it turns, das where the gangs shacks are. It's ten of dem. Den, down dee road a short ways is where Vinny lives wit five teen girls. He's a monster."

I slowed the truck and looked in my rear view mirror. There were two trucks following me that held members of the Duffle Bag Cartel. Glancing over to the shacks that she was talking about, I noticed smoke coming from the roofs of them. "Shawty, you sure that's where his crew lives?"

"Jess, I am."

"What are the odds he's there with them right now?" Smoke asked, looking back at her.

She shrugged her shoulders. "Don't know. I am here wit you." She frowned and sat back in her seat looking irritated.

I scanned the area. It seemed to be infested with prostitutes of all ages, shapes, and sizes. They walked up and down the dirt road flagging down cars. Once the cars pulled to the side of the road they got inside of them, and the cars pulled away. There were two street lamps that did very little to illuminate the area. I was thankful for that. "Well, ma'am, I know they took your sons away from you, and I'm sorry to hear that. It seems like y'all have a problem with infestation here, but don't worry, we finna exterminate these rats. You hear me?"

"Jess, and tank you so much. Dey is da devils."

***

I made sure that my mask was situated properly over my face and tightened the silencer on my guns. Without wasting any more time, I opened the door to the truck, and softly closed it back, before jogging toward the metal shacks with Smoke, and a few members from the Cartel close behind.

The Puerto Rican woman had more heart, or should I say more hate, in her heart than I realized. She held an empty flour sack in her hand and played things real cool. She'd decided to help us by acting as if she needed to borrow flour from each shack that we were set to run inside. That way it would be easier for us to get them to open the door. I was cool with the plot as long as we were able to handle our business in an orderly fashion. She told us to wait for the code word before we attacked. The code word would be, Gracias.

She walked up to the first shack and knocked on the door. We waited on the side of it with our guns silenced, ready to blow. When it opened, she started speaking Spanish real fast. Somebody responded to her. She held up the bag to show them it was empty. There appeared to be a lot of angry grumbling. She held up the bag again, and then nodded, held up a hand. "Esta bien. Gracias." With that being said, she stepped back, and to the side.

I took that as my cue. I jumped up and pressed the barrel of my Forty Five to the eye of the big, buff, dude that was standing in the doorway. He tensed up but it was too late. "Welcome to Memphis, muthafucka!" *Boof.*

His brains blew out of the back of his head, before he fell to the ground in a heap of flesh and bones. Smoke jumped over him, and so did the rest of our Cartel, with guns out. I rushed inside behind them.

The shack shocked the shit out of me. It was packed with big screen televisions and top notch appliances. It looked like a man cave more than anything else. Another plus was that it appeared we'd caught the majority of them off guard. Everywhere I looked there was somebody scrambling. My gun was blasting back to back, knocking holes in everything that was trying to run, with no remorse.

Smoke let both of his guns ride. They chopped down one Rican after the next. The end result was a shack full of dead bodies, and a stream of blood that flowed toward the front door of the shack, probably because the village was built on a hill.

We rushed out of there and it was more of the same in the next three shacks. Guns were emptied and reloaded. Bodies dropped like rain from the sky. I saw so many head shots that it wasn't funny. One thing for sure and that's that the Duffle Bag Cartel had not come to play games.

114

When we got back in the truck the Puerto Rican woman had a big smile in her face. "Now Vinny. You just must get Vinny. I'll take you to he home. He's there wit Vanessa. Don't kill Vanessa. She my daughter." She said this looking directly at me.

I nodded. "I got you, ma'."

Smoke turned around. "You let him spend time wit your daughter after what he did to your sons. That's nuts." He shook his head.

"Is dee only way to trap him. She thirteen. He like li'l girls. She dare, he won't leave. Told him she virgin. Small price to pay for revenge."

"Yeah, I get it ,shawty. We gon handle this ma'fucka for you. Maybe when we get around here you can knock on the door and ask to speak to your li'l girl. Once he open that door, we in that bitch. You see how we get down." I said, feeling my heart beating harder and harder in my chest.

"Maybe you stay here and protect us from people like dem. You save our peoples."

"I don't know about all that shawty. We got too much on our plate already. We'll take care of one thing at a time. Let's make this happen."

We pulled to the back of Vinny's shack three minutes later. Coincidentally, where his shack was located there wasn't a single light in sight. It was pitch black all around for at least half a block. We surrounded the shack. The Puerto Rican woman, Smoke and myself went around to the front door. We ducked down and prepared for her to knock. Before her knuckles could touch the door, there was a loud scream that was emitted from the inside. Silence, and then a slap, followed by another scream.

The Puerto Rican lady beat on the door. She spoke Spanish. There was more beating on the door. She appeared to be in a frenzy. She tried to look in the side window with no success. The enraged mother rushed back over to the front door and started to beat again, screaming in Spanish. And beating the door with both fists.

The door swung inward. Vinny appeared with a naked girl. He held her by the hair with one hand and had a big knife in his other. When he saw the Puerto Rican female, he frowned and snapped in Spanish.

She dropped to her knees and appeared to be praying to him, begging and pleading in Spanish. The little girl that he held cried. Her lip was busted and one of her eyes blackened.

Vinny flung her into the house, kicked the little girl in the ass, and cursed at her in Spanish again. He turned to what had to be her mother. He grabbed her by the throat and sliced it two quick times before I could even stand up. She dropped to the ground, choking on her own blood.

"Nooooooo!" The girl screamed.

Vinny turned around to assault her. He knelt, and grabbed a handful of her hair, all the while cursing in Spanish.

Before he could pick her up, Smoke was on his ass. He slammed the piece into the back of Vinny's head and knocked him inside of the house. "Bitch ass nigga! Remember me?"

Vinny fell on his back and hopped right back up. There were five naked girls inside the shack that screamed and ran for cover. Vinny brandished the knife. "Come on, muthafucka. Come on!"

The rest of the Cartel stepped into the small house and posted up. I held them back. I knew Smoke could handle this in his own. He didn't need any help. Besides, I wanted him to enjoy what he was about to do to Vinny. "Nobody moves. Smoke fuck him over."

Vinny motioned for him to come on. "Let's go, mutha-fucka. Come on." He swiped at Smoke with the knife.

Smoke jumped back. He took his mask off of his face and tossed it to me. "Hold this, bruh."

I caught it and tucked it into my pocket. "Handle yo bidness, li'l homie. Give that ma'fucka a taste of the Mound."

Smoke smiled. "I am." He turned and fired.

Boof. Boof.

The shots knocked both of Vinny's knee caps off of him.

Vinny fell to the floor. "Aww. Aww. You son of a bitch!" He struggled to get up. His knife slid across the floor.

Smoke kicked him as hard as he could in the chest. Vinny flew into a table, knocking over the bottles of liquor that were on top of it. Smoke picked up Vinny's knife. "You had the nerve to knock my teeth out of my mouth." He rushed Vinny and kicked him in the chest again. This time the blow was so hard that I literally saw his ribs cave inward on one side.

Vinny crawled to his knees, then stood up. "Drop the knife. Fight me like a man, you filthy nigger. Fight me!"

Smoke rushed him again and punched Vinny with his right hand and sliced him across the cheek with the knife in his left. Blood skeeted across the wall.

Vinny stumbled backward. His back wound up against the wall. He dabbed at the blood with his fingers and rubbed them together. His fluid ran down his face and dripped off of his chin. He clenched his teeth and hollered. "Arrrggh!" Vinny ran at Smoke with his head down.

Smoke side stepped him and sliced him three quick times across the face. He poked him in the back five times and grabbed him around the neck. "Huh Phoenix, finish this Bitch nigga for me, bruh. You still the head, and this punk offended you too." He held the knife out for me.

I put both guns on my hip and took the knife from him. He held Vinny in a full Nelson. I didn't waste any time . I remembered how I felt watching him and his crew rob me and Smoke. Mentally, I flashed back to how he'd beat Smoke's grill in before taking the gold from his mouth and dropping it into a bag as if it was the most natural thing in the world. Yeah, he had to pay for all of that. I slammed the knife into his face and ripped it downward. A huge gash formed. Blood gushed out of it like a busted fire hydrant.

Smoke dropped him to the ground. We watched him crawl, and flop around on the floor.

I handed Smoke the knife. "Gon head and finish him, bruh, so we can get up out of here."

"Say no mo'." Smoke sat on Vinny's back, pulled his head back and sawed through his throat until his knife made it from one side to the other. He stood up looking down on him. "Straight fuck nigga, Phoenix. On every-thang, mane."

Chapter 14

After we put that fuck nigga Vinny to sleep, I felt it was time for us to get up off of the island. It was hot as hell and flooded with law enforcement. They were already talking about putting the whole city of San Juan on lock down because so many people had lost their lives in one night. I was afraid that if we didn't get out if there soon that we were going to get jammed up. That would've been the worst thing to take place because I just sensed that the jails in Puerto Rico had to be hell.

On the night before we were set to leave, Sabrina came into the bedroom as I was rocking my daughter Shantê to sleep. I'd spent the entire day with Shantê catering to her every need. We watched one Disney movie after the next, until finally it seemed as if her battery was running low. She struggled to keep her eyes open. I kissed her cheek and held mine against her own looking up at Sabrina.

Sabrina wore a short, red, negligee that stopped at the top of her thighs. Whenever she moved in the slightest it showed off the bottom swells of her globes. She rubbed lotion into her arms, smiled at me then held one finger in the air and gave me the, 'come here signal'.

Shantê had drifted off. I laid her on the bed and kissed her forehead again. Then, I slowly made my way out of the bed, before tucking her in. When I made my way to Sabrina she was standing with her back against the dresser. The scent of her Prada perfume met me before I was standing in her face.

She moved closer and rested her nose against mine. Her light brown eyes peered into my own. "This is our last night in Puerto Rico Phoenix. You got a way to send us off in style?" She licked her thick lips.

I lowered my head. Pulled her to me. My hands ducked under and cupped that ass. It was fully exposed, hot to the touch and soft. "You already know what's on my mind. What, you ready to come around?" I teased.

She giggled and looked past my shoulder. "You gave Shantê everything she wanted today. She went on damn near every ride at that li'l carnival. She should be down for the count for a nice long while. Come on, let's go in your room and get it in." She sucked my bottom lip into her mouth and slipped her tongue inside. Sabrina grabbed the back of my neck and breathed heavily as we made out with forbidden lust.

I picked her up as she wrapped her thighs around me. I carried her out into the hallway of the suite, locked my daughter's door, then walked right across the hallway, and slipped my key card into the door before pushing it open. The whole time we were kissing and going crazy all over one another.

When I got inside the room the lights were turned off, but there were lit candles everywhere I looked. Natalia stood in the middle of the floor dressed in a short, white lingerie fit, with the garter belt, and white stockings. Her heels were red Louboutin's. "I hope there is room for one more." She walked toward us all sexy like, with her slightly bowed legs.

Sabrina slipped out of my arms. "Phoenix, when was you gon tell me that she was Taurus's daughter? That she was our family?" She walked up to Natalia and hugged her and brushed her pretty hair out of her face.

Natalia slipped her hands around Sabrina's waist cupping her juicy ass and moaned. "I swear I love our family so much. What better way to leave Puerto Rico with a bang?" She tilted her head sideways. Her and Sabrina were making out loudly, moaning into each other's faces.

My dick got rock hard right away. I stepped behind Sabrina and started to strip her. When I pulled the straps of her negligee off of her shoulders it dropped to the floor. And she stepped out of it. I knelt down and kissed all over her pretty booty while I rubbed her pussy from behind. To make the moment last, I sniffed my fingers nice and slow before sucking them into my mouth. Then I was playing with Sabrina's hot spot again. Both Natalia's fingers and my own were in her gap.

"Unnnn. Unnnn. This damn family. This damn family." Sabrina spread her feet apart. She and Natalia became involved in an erotic battle of the tongues. They were sucking all over each other's faces and tongues.

After a while Sabrina wound up sitting in the middle of the bed with both me and Natalia between her legs. I held one pussy lip, and Natalia held open the other one. We took turns sucking on her pearl tongue, fingering her pussy and sucking her juices off of each other's lips.

"Oh. Oh. Oh. Yes. Eat me. Eat it, cuz. Fuck yes. Fuck yes. Unnnn, shit yes." Sabrina laid on her back and squeezed her pretty titties together. The nipples were poked out like pinkies. She pulled on them and tried to fit them into her mouth. It looked so good.

I fingered her pussy fast. Natalia kept her lips wrapped around her clitoris while I did so. Sabrina reached under herself and played with her own pussy. From time to time my fingers would wind up in her gap as well, fingering while she humped backward into my digits. The entire time her pussy hole was tightening around them.

Sabrina opened her thighs as wide as they could go. She watched as we brought her to the brink of her climax as a team, Natalia sucking, and me diving into her pussy as far as my digits could reach. Faster and faster. Her kitty started making noises, queefing and squirting juices out her tight hole. "I'm cumin cuz. I'm cumin. Aw. Aw. Ohhhhhhh! Yesssss! Shit." She started to buck her ass forward into my fingers, and Natalia's mouth.

Natalia moved me out of the way. She was eating Sabrina so good that I started to jack my dick watching them. It looked so hot with Natalia's thick ass in the air. Her yellow pussy was engorged and leaking. It was slightly parted because of the way she was bent. I could hear her slurping all over Sabrina's box.

I stuck my face in Natalia's gap and licked up and down her groove. Without missing a beat, I opened her gates, and stuck my tongue inside of her. Her clit was poked out just as far as Sabrina's. As crazy at it may sound, they even tasted alike. That drove me nuts. I stood up and slid into Natalia. I had to have some of that pussy. I grabbed her hips and started killing that shit too. My dick opened her hole right up. Her womb sucked at me hungrily.

She was eating Sabrina even more than before. Sabrina got on all fours holding her cheeks apart while Natalia licked every inch of her crack. When she focused in on her clit again, and sucked it into her lips, Sabrina went crazy. She was beating her fist on the bed and screaming. "Uhh. Uhhh. Yesssss. Yesssss!" Her face fell to the bed. She started to cum for the second time.

I smacked Natalia on the ass , pounded into her from the back, long stroking that pussy. She looked over her shoulder. Her face was shiny and greasy from Sabrina's secretions. It looked so good to me that it sent tingles up and down my spine. I dug in harder and faster. In one quick move, I sucked my middle finger and slipped it into

Natalia's pink back door. She yelped. Her pussy walls tightened around my dick. "Natalia, shit baby. Shit. I'm cumming." Spasms rocked me as I came back to back in her pussy.

Sabrina screamed again. She forced Natalia's head into her box. "I'm cumin, cuz. Aw fuck, this bitch know how to eat pussy. I swear she do. Unnnn! Shit." She collapsed to her stomach. Her hand slipped under her stomach and wound up in her crotch.

Natalia bent down and opened her ass. She licked all around her rose bud. Her tongue dipped in and out of it faster and faster.

I flipped Sabrina on her side, lifted her thick thigh in the air, and slid into her pussy. My big dick head burrowed its way inside of her hot body. I cocked back and slammed it home and repeated the process faster each time I entered her.

"Phoenix. Phoenix. Phoenix. Li'l cuz. Aw. Aw. Aw. Fuck me. Li'l cuz. Fuck me. Ooo. Ooo. Yes. Shit yes. Mmm-hm!"

Natalia sat cross legged on the bed and fingered her own pussy. Every so often she would pull her fingers out and suck them into her mouth, then it was right back to fingering herself. "Fuck her harder, Phoenix. It's your job. Unnnn." More fingering. She pinched her own clit. "It's your job to take care of us. You're all we got." She laid her face on Sabrina's hip and licked all over it. Her fingers continued to go to work between her thighs. She held them out to me. I sucked them clean. She returned them to her box and groaned.

"Cum in me Phoenix. Cum in me like you used to do when we were kids. Uhhh! Yes baby."

I remembered how we used to be under Sabrina's bed screwing away while her brother and sister slept a short distance across the room. I'd be feeling all over her barely there breasts that were mostly nipples. Her tight coochie would milk me until I couldn't take it no more.

"Huh. Huh. Huh. Huh." I squeezed her ass hard. Slammed into it and came hard. Thinking to myself how I'd just nutted in both of their of pussies in the same night. That was living for me.

Sabrina forced Natalia to the bed on her back. She opened her sex lips and rubbed them up and down hers. Their clits wrestled against one another. I knelt and pumped my piece while I watched them go at it.

"I'm part of this family too. Unnnn. Love me. Yes. Love me Sabrina." Natalia groaned opening her thighs wider.

Sabrina sucked Natalia's neck, reached between them and played with her pussy. She slid two of them into her and beat it up. "We love you cuz. We love you too. Unn. You're a part of this family." She flipped her on to her stomach, and humped her ass, after spreading her own pussy lips. Sabrina grabbed her hips and humped as if she was fucking her like a savage.

My hand was between both of their legs. Both pussies were dripping wetter then I had ever seen them before. It was amazing.

Natalia screamed, and came all over Sabrina's box. They lay hugged up kissing and sucking all over one another for the next ten minutes.

After they finished they took turns riding me at full speed. One would cum and slide off. Then the other would get up there and ride me until she couldn't hold back any longer. We wound up fucking into the wee hours of the morning.

***

First thing in the morning Sabrina woke me up by pushing on my chest. "Phoenix. Phoenix. Get yo ass up. I can't find Shantê!" She screamed.

"What?!" I sat up in a panic. Jumped out of the bed and nearly knocked Natalia on the floor.

"You heard what I said. I can't find Shantê. She's not in the room." She had tear streaks on her cheeks.

Natalia sat up. The sheets fell off of her breasts. "What's going on?"

"I can't find Shantê and I'm freaking out." Sabrina shrieked.

Ghost

Chapter 15

"Man, y'all tripping, bruh. You know damn well I wasn't about to let nothin happen to Princess Shantê. I came to this doe at about five in the morning and y'all was in here getting it in. I heard so much moaning and groaning that I thought somebody was in here dying. Li'l shawty stuck her head out of the room just as I was coming from knocking on the door. She looked scared, so I snatched her up. I left you a text bruh. You and Sabrina." Smoke said, sipping from his apple juice.

Sabrina paced back and forth. "You can't be doing shit like that Smoke. She's already been taken from us once. Man, I literally lost my mind when I went in that room and she was nowhere to be found. Damn, I felt so guilty."

Natalia sighed, and hugged Shantê. "Well, from here on out I'll keep a security team on her at all times to make sure that nothing happens to our Princess. She means to much to all of us."

I was sitting on the couch feeling like shit. Instead of making sure that my daughter was safe and sound I was too busy chasing pussy. That had always been my problem. Pussy was my biggest addiction. Forbidden pussy that was. My obsession with that could have caused me to lose my daughter had Smoke been anybody other than who he was.

Shantê slipped out of Natalia's grasp, and sat on my lap. She wrapped one arm around my neck, kissed my cheek. "It's okay, daddy. I was only with Uncle Smoke. He took me to a taco place that had a playground. It was pretty cool. I didn't think you would get mad at me." She whispered and rubbed the side of my face.

"I'm not mad at you, baby. I'm mad at me. Daddy should of did things differently. From here on out, I will." I hugged her little body and kissed her cheek again.

Smoke stood up. "Y'all tripping. All of y'all. Li'l mama good. I had her. Ain't that right, Princess?" He smiled his jewelry filled mouth at her.

She blushed. "Yeah, that's right." Then her face was in my chest.

Smoked laughed. "So, what time we dipping up out of here?" He took a swig of his apple juice.

"There is a few people that I want you and Phoenix to sit down and meet with. After the meeting, we're in the skies. We'll stop in Memphis to take care of the unfinished business there, and then we're off to an island of some sort. Me and Phoenix haven't exactly figured that part of things out yet. But, as soon as we do, the people in this room will be the first to know."

Smoke looked from Natalia to me. "Y'all saying that I'ma be able to go too?"

I felt offended. "Bruh, you my li'l homie. We got the whole state of Tennessee kicking down doors looking for us. What kind of nigga would I be if I broke ties with you now that the pressure is on?" I stood up and gave him a half hug.

"That's why I fuck wit you, Phoenix. You always been one hunnit, bruh. Thorough. Through and through. We definitely gotta get our people out of Memphis. It ain't safe. I was hoping that cousin Natalia could arrange for somebody to scoop my shorties, and maybe one of my baby mothers. It's already gon be risky enough trying to get in there and handle Mikey and get back out. You feel me?"

Natalia came over and took my hand. She interlocked our fingers. "That's something else that me and Phoenix can talk about. But right now, we need to get you guys ready to meet a heavy hitter in the game. Phoenix you remember that talk that we had about the South right?"

I nodded. I wanted to conquer the whole damn thang. Memphis was starting to look real small to me. Besides, if I could make damn near five hundred thousand in a day in small ass Memphis, I knew that I could make fifty million in a week if I had the entire South, if not more. The jury was still out on that. "Yeah shawty. I remember."

"Well, if anybody is going to put you in the position that you speak of, it's Kilroy. He's a major power player in the game, and he's looking for someone to invest his power and leverage into. If the meeting goes well, we could look to be in business with him within the next ninety days or so. So, you guys should get your game plan together. I think this is a major opportunity for you, Phoenix. What do you think?"

"You still only gave me a brief run down as to who this stud is. I'm trusting your guidance on this one. If you thinking it's the right decision for us, then that's what we'll do. Set it up, and me and li'l bruh gon see what's good. Aiight?"

She smiled and nodded. "Will do. After we meet with him we'll be on our way. Then we'll head over to Memphis, and finish what was started there, and it'll be over with. Sounds good."

"Sounds good." I returned.

***

After doing a li'l digging, I was able to find out that Kilroy was a major kingpin type nigga from Philadelphia. He had his hands in everything that came across the borders of the United States. Apparently, before Nastia was killed she'd also supplied him with bricks and bricks of the Rebirth. He and my uncle Taurus was supposed to have some sort of connection, and that was another reason why Natalia wanted me and him to hook up.

In just under five years, Kilroy had taken the product that Nastia supplied him with and managed to flood the entire east coast. He went from strictly handling the Rebirth to everythang else. Now, supposedly, he was in every major city out East, in the Midwest cities, and slowly making his way backward toward California. Natalia said that he'd had his sights in the southern states for a long time but had yet to find any real investors to put him time and leverage behind. I paid attention as she spoke for over an hour about what she'd learned about him and picked up along the way from dealing with him. I couldn't wait to meet him. Anybody that got Natalia talking the way that he did had to be someone special. When it came to men she rarely ever raved about them.

She sat on the bed beside me and took my hand into her own. "Baby, you know you don't have to do this right? I mean I got you. For as long as I am alive, you never have to pick up a fuckin drug or anything negative. I got us. Does that mean anything to you?"

I shook my head. "Nall. I already told you that I'm my own man. I can't sit back and let you do everything. I need my own kingdom, my own legacy. If fuckin wit Kilroy is step one, then that's what it is."

She looked at me for a long time and sighed. "Okay then. We meet him in an hour. I'll finish getting dressed."

***

For the meeting they had shut down a boardroom at some law firm right off of the business district. Me, Smoke, Natalia, and our security waited in that room for a full hour before Kilroy showed up with an entourage of angry look-ing animals. He stopped at the head of the table, and his goons filed inside of the room and surrounded it. They were strapped with assault rifles, with masks on their faces.

Natalia got up and walked over to him. He opened his arms and gave her a hug, and his big hands trailed down to her waist just above her ass. The closer he got to her round derrière the madder it made me. I didn't realize how jealous I was, when it came to her, until then. He kissed her on both cheeks and stood back holding her right hand. "My, my, my," the heavy set, dark skinned man said, looking her up and down. "Girl, if yo daddy could see you now he'd try and murder any nigga that looked at you. Word to the gods, man. This is perfection." He made her turn in a circle while he held her hand over her head.

Natalia laughed, and took her hand away. "Thank you, Kilroy. Now there are some guys here that I want you to meet. She switched as she stepped to the side of my chair. I noted that his eyes were all over her ass. That further in-furiated me. I didn't like the way his punk ass was peeping my shawty. I didn't care what our relationship was. In my mind, she was my bitch. I was sure she was in her mind as well. "This is my cousin, Phoenix. He's Taurus's nephew." She made sure that she threw that part in there as an added incentive.

I stood up and extended my hand. "What's good, bruh?"

Kilroy stepped around to my side of the table and stopped in front of me. He looked into my eyes, then sized me up. "You the nigga that been making all of that noise in Memphis? You got the whole state of Tennessee on fire like arson kid. Word up. Yo, that ain't the way we gon get this money by the barrel. I'm letting you know that right now." He took my hand and squeezed it so hard that I wanted to punch him in his shit.

I pulled my hand back and mugged him. "Say, Playboy, you ain't gotta squeeze my hand all hard and shit." I wiggled the fingers on my right hand and felt it over with my left.

Kilroy laughed. "You can tell everything about a man from his handshake. Yours needs to be tighter. You talking about taking over the South, you're going to be rubbing elbows with a lot of power players that will be judging your handshake, and which way to deal wit you because of it. The smallest things in the game will tell a heavy hitter what kind of nigga you are. Never forget that."

"Man, they gon see how I organize and get this money. Fuck a handshake. I couldn't care less if I never shook another nigga's hand for the rest if my life. That's what that is right there, shawty." I looked him up and down. I ain't like this East coast muthafucka already. He had my hand throbbing.

He frowned and looked as if he were about to say something. Then smiled. "Yeah, I can see that Taurus shit in you. Who is this right here?" He asked nodding toward Smoke.

"This my right hand man, Smoke. Bruh is as thorough as they come. We eat off the same plate, with the same portions."

He brushed past me and held his hand out to Smoke. "What's good, li'l homie?"

Smoke stood up and balled his fist. "Ain't nothing, shawty. What's to it?"

Kilroy looked his fist over and laughed. He dapped him and headed back to the front of the table. "That's a smart man right there." He took a seat. "Y'all sit down and get comfortable. We gon be here for a minute."

We followed suit.

Kilroy looked around the room. "Natalia, do you swear by these two?"

She nodded. "I told you, they are my family. I swear by both of them. You said you were looking for a crew of hungry animals to invade the South, well my cousin Phoenix here and his Duffle Bag Cartel are the animals you seek. I stand behind him one hundred percent."

"Duffle Bag Cartel, huh?" Kilroy, pulled a cigar out of his inside coat pocket, and sparked the end of it. "Well, one thing this Cartel should know is that if you get in the bed with me, I'll be the one calling the shots. I'll be the one pulling the strings. What I say goes. Is that going to be a problem?"

"Hell yeah. As far as I'm concerned I'm my own man. We built this Cartel from the slums up. Ain't no mutha-fucka finna just come in and think that he sits on of the throne. That's my seat. I don't mind coming to the table and moving as a unit but falling under you. Fuck that." I stood up. "Let's roll, y'all."

All around the room Kilroy's men began to cock their straps. They took one step forward, making it seem like they were ready to strike. Kilroy looked into my eyes and smiled. "I think you might wanna take a seat, homeboy. We got a lot of talking to do, besides, I think you're over reacting."

Natalia placed her hand on my shoulder. "Just hear him out, Phoenix. There is nothing wrong wit listening."

Smoke had his hand under his shirt. "I don't give a fuck what you gots to say, Kilroy. I fuck wit Phoenix the long way. He built this Cartel. We buss these guns for the Homie. That's what it is."

Kilroy frowned. "So, you'll die for this nigga, then?"

"In a heart beat." Smoke assured him.

"And Phoenix, would you die for him." Kilroy asked me.

"You muthafuckin right. That's my nigga." I said mugging him.

"That's half the battle right there. I've studied you niggas a li'l bit. I already know y'all bout that life. I even got word about how y'all handled Vinny and his crew out here. I like what I've heard thus far. All we gotta do is clean up those mistakes in Memphis, and I'm sure we can do bidness. Besides, you got Taurus' blood in you. Natalia is standing behind you. That's a lot of power to work wit. I say you have a seat and let's figure this thang out. I'm sure we can come to an agreement on this to get us all filthy rich by conquering the south."

Before the meeting was over we sure did.

Chapter 16

Kilroy made it plain and simple, if he was going to stand behind us, we'd have to finish what we'd started in the city of Memphis first. That meant we had to crush Mikey, and his crew. The problem with the authorities could be taken care of in another way, at another time. Kilroy said to leave all of that to politics. I didn't know what that meant, but I was sure that the police weren't about to forgo the knowledge of what me and Smoke were supposed to have done. Either way, that wasn't my primary focus. It was time to get rid of Mikey and close that loose end.

We left Puerto Rico early the next morning and landed in Memphis later that afternoon. We'd dropped off Sabrina and Shanté in Miami, Florida with a shit load of security that Natalia had put in place for them. As soon as the wheels hit the runway, I got a bunch of butterflies in my stomach. I knew I was home, but, at the same time, being home for me meant that it was time to go into action. One glance over to Smoke told me that he was thinking the same thing.

He looked nervous, as he peered out of the window and shook his head. "Man, if it was up to me I would of never came back to this bitch. Mane, we stupid as hell for stepping foot in this state again. Ain't nothing good can come from us being back here. I hope you know that, bruh." He turned up the bottle of Moët he was drinking.

I knew he was right, but I was stubborn. There was no part of me that could go on with my life knowing that Mikey had breath in his body. He had to pay for what he'd done to Shanté, and he had to pay for the slugs he put in my body. There was no way around that shit. "Mane, we just gon handle this bidness and get up out if here. It's as simple as that."

Smoke sighed and took another long swallow. "Like I said before homie, I'm riding wit you until the dirt. If you bout that life, then I'm gone be about that life right beside you. But, in my personal opinion, this is suicide, pure and simple."

I scoffed and let my seat back a tad. Natalia rubbed the side of my face and kissed my cheek. "Baby, before you guys get ready to go where you're going, I wanna show you something that might change your mind. We're going to make a pit stop. Cool?"

I looked her over from the corner of my eye. I didn't know what she had up her sleeve, but I'm sure I was set to find out. "That's cool, baby. Gimme some."

She leaned into me and kissed my lips. "I got you, daddy. No matter what you decide to do. I got you."

***

Smoke stepped into the door of the empty duplex apartment and looked around. "Mane, this a nice ass crib right here. You telling me you only use this for a storage space?" He asked Natalia.

She shrugged her shoulders and finished punching in the numbers on the ADT system. "In this business that one thing you'll learn is that looks can be deceiving, and that most things are not what they appear to be. Case in point, me. Do I look like I am as lethal as I really am?" She turned and batted her eye lashes at the both of us, looking oh so sexy.

I looked her up and down and nodded my approval at that beauty. Natalia got finer and finer to me every single day. "Lethal, huh?"

"Yeah, lethal." She returned.

Smoke smacked his lips. "Lethal? Man, shawty quit playing. You can't pass for lethal. You might have Tarus' blood in you, but that don't make you a killa."

She smiled. "That's what I was going for. As long as a man judges a woman based on of her looks, and not her strengths, women will always be the most strong and dominant. There is nothing that you guys are about to do that you won't need my help in assisting you to accomplish. Things are not about to be as easy as you think they are. Follow me." She waved us forward.

Smoke raised his right eye brow, and looked over at me. "Yo, that's yo peoples right there, Potna."

My eyes were glued to the back of Natalia's Prada jeans. They cupped her ass so righteously. I felt like jumping on top of her ass and ripping them off and fucking her as hard as I could, but I had to change my focus. There were many tasks at hand. "That's my baby, li'l homie. We gotta respect her role right now."

"Tell em again, daddy." Natalia swished down the hallway and stopped at a door on the right side that had a combination lock on the outside of it. "First things first, you're going to need weapons." She clicked the lock and pulled it off, then she moved the latch that held the lock, and pushed the door in. She stepped inside and moved to the side.

I saw green crate after crate. Each one said: United States Military Personnel Only. The lids were taken off of them, inside of the crates were a bunch of military issued weapons. There were hand guns, assault rifles, knives, and even grenades.

Smoke rushed over and picked up a grenade. He looked Natalia up and down and smiled. "Shawty, you ain't holding like this, I know." He cheesed his golden smile.

"Looks can be deceiving, right?" She said while looking into my eyes.

I picked up one of the M-16s and looked through the scope and zoomed it in in the wall. The vision was so good that I could see a tiny crack. The gun felt light in my hands. I knew I wouldn't have a problem running and gunning with it. "No matter how lethal you are, baby, it ain't gon stop you from being bad." I joked.

She rolled her eyes. "You guys should be able to put these things to good use. Each one comes equipped with a hundred round clip, infrared beam, and you're able to break it down and get rid if it in sections. This is some twenty nineteen, upgraded material for your ass. Or should I say their asses, because they're going to reap the repercussions from it. Those grenades having an eight second detonation sequence. Remember that because you have up to six seconds to throw them, and another two before you need to get at least a safe fifty feet away. They're small but they pack a heavy punch." She picked one up and pulled out the pin.

Both me and Smoke ran into the hallway. You could hear the sounds if our shoes scuffling on the floor. I even farted a li'l bit in my haste to get the fuck out of that room.. "Natalia, what's wrong with you?" I hollered.

She stepped into the hallway, looking down at her pink Rolex. She seemed to be counting the seconds. Then she casually placed the pin back inside if it's and tossed it at our feet. "Here."

I jumped so high in the air that I bumped my head on the ceiling, came down and broke camp toward the front of the house. My heart was pounding in my chest.

Smoke beat me to the front door. He opened it and rushed outside . "Mane, shawty a li'l too crazy for me, Potna. She playing wit grenades and shit. No way."

Natalia slapped her thick thighs and made them jiggle inside of her tight jeans. She busted up laughing and fell to her knees, laughing so hard that her yellow face was red as a strawberry. Tears squeezed out of her eyes. "Oh my God. Uh. Uh. Damn. I ain't never seen nobody run that fast in my life. That was some gold metal, Olympic shit right there. Uh. Uh." She bent over and continued to bust a gut.

I stepped back inside and looked down on her. "Say, shawty, that shit wasn't funny. You about to make me have a heart attack."

Smoke stepped into the house and closed the door. "I'm starting to think her li'l, fine ass is out of her mind. Playing wit some shit that could kill all of us." He frowned and mugged her with anger.

She pulled herself up by using the wall. "Uh. Uh. Shit. That was funny. Okay. Okay. Damn. My stomach hurts. Ooo it hurts so bad." Natalia was rolling again, louder than before.

"Man!" Smoke started.

She had me laughing now, and I was angry as hell. At least I was trying to be. "Come on baby with this bull shit. We gotta move to the next phase of things. Knock it off."

She nodded, and stood up, wiping the tears from her eyes. "Aiight. Damn. Y'all so sensitive. Come on." She picked up the grenade from the floor and tossed it up and down. Natalia went back into the artillery room and dropped it inside of the crate along with the rest of them. "Anyway, now you see the eight second thing is factual. I replaced the pin when there was two seconds left. Alright, now let's go to the next room." She stepped out of that one and headed down the hallway. As we came to the room at the far of it, Natalia grabbed the lock spun the combination, and removed it. "Phoenix, this is what it looks like when I have a bunch of hustlers doing for me what you are trying to have your crew doing. This is why I am telling you we don't need to do this." She said walking to the far end of the empty room and rolling the closet door to the side. I followed closed behind her. She tapped the wall, and it fell inward. "Can I get some help please?"

I rushed over and took a hold of the big, blue trunk, grabbed a handle and pulled it with all of my might. Smoke came around and helped me to get the trunk into the middle of the room. It felt like it weighed a million pounds, but we got it there.

Natalia stood in front of the trunk for a second and sighed before popping the latches on it and pulling open the top. Inside of it was filled with stacks and stacks of cash. Every bill that I saw was either a hundred or a fifty. It was crazy.

"What the fuck? How much money is that?" I asked picking up a few stacks and thumbing through them. Sure, enough it was all hundreds and fifties.

"I don't know. Should be around a million dollars, easily though. I ain't had the time to have it counted."

Smoke's eyes were wide open. "Damn, shawty, you don't even know how much this is supposed to be. Now that makes you lethal. Phoenix, I wish she was my cousin. Shawty plugged like a muthafucka and she bad." He looked her over with lust in his eyes.

"Well, I'm not. And only Phoenix can get a taste of this, so you can quit looking like you're about to salivate at the mouth. It's only going to hurt you in the long run." She glared at him, and I knew she was serious.

Smoke held up his hands. "Whoa, shawty. I was just looking. I like that rich girl shit. It's alluring, but I'd never try and overstep my bounds. I know what it is wit you and Phoenix. That's my nigga."

"Long as you know." She looked up at me. "Baby, now that I've taken over my mother's operations, I'm getting drop offs like this every single day in certain locations throughout the United States. There is no reason for you to be in the streets hustling when I'm in complete love with you. You're my everything."

Damn, she was striking a cord wit my heart and shit. It was hard to not go there wit Natalia. On some real shit I knew that I was falling in love with her too, but it was still weird to me. After all we were family, no amount of love could ever change that fact. "Natalia, I already told you what it was. The sight of this money ain't enough to knock me off the path of getting my own shit. We can discuss this at another time though. For now, we gon snatch up those weapons and get this show on the road first thing in the morning."

Smoke eyed the money. "Damn that's a million dollars, and she saying she get bundles like this on a daily basis? Fuck you lucky Phoenix. It's niggas that a kill to be in your position."

I shot daggers at him. "It's all good nigga. Me and her gon figure this out. You just focus on how we finna cut these niggas throats out tomorrow."

Smoke nodded. "Will do. Matter fact let me make some phone calls. I'ma give y'all a minute to talk." He stepped out of the room and closed the door.

"I'm pregnant Phoenix."

"What?" I dropped the stacks on money on the hardwood floor.

"I said I'm pregnant. Nine weeks. It's yours. I mean ours and I'm keeping it. I love you so fucking much."

Fuck n'all. I knew I hadn't slipped up like that and gotten Natalia pregnant. What the fuck was I thinking. I felt sick on the stomach all of the sudden. "Natalia, baby we're cousins we can't have no child together, what if...?"

"We're not siblings Phoenix. It's not like our baby is going to come out with eight arms and legs. It's going to be perfectly healthy. Don't start to freak out over that. It's the least of our worries. We need to decide what you're going to do about the game? Or even this whole revenge thing. I think you need to let it go. We need to move on with our lives and raise our family. You and I." She stepped in front of me and kissed my lips and slid her arms around my neck.

I cupped that ass. It was the only way I could hold her. She was so thick. To be honest the more I thought about her being pregnant it didn't really bother me. I had a thing for Natalia as bad as she had for me. In fact, I think mine was getting worse. "Baby you know what, I'm glad that you're pregnant. I just pray that our shawty comes out healthy, and as beautiful as her mother."

"Or his father. What are you saying, that you want another girl?"

"N'all, a son would be just as good. Long as he's healthy."

"And the game, and revenge. What about those two things?"

I sighed. "The revenge can't wait. I gotta handle by bidness with Mikey. He hurt my daughter. He put slugs in my body. And when it comes to the game, I can handle my bidness through Smoke.

I would love to see him shine. Li'l homie is a good dude. He got a couple of kids that need his support. He gotta get is riches all the way up. If I can help him do that then it'll make me feel like it's me that's still in the game even if I'm just somewhere laid up with you from afar." My eye trailed down to hers.

She squealed. "So, you're saying you're going to leave it alone? That you're going to be a family with me and our child that's on the way?" I could hear the excitement in her voice. On top of that she was shaking like crazy.

"Yeah, baby, that's what I'm saying. I'm saying I'll step off of the grinding battle field of the game, and I'll simply handle my part from somewhere on a yacht next to you, and our children. Once a man becomes a king he no longer does the day by day things that he used to. That's what he has workers, and underlings for."

She jumped up and down and wrapped her arms around my neck. "Oh daddy, you make me so happy. So so happy. We're going to have the best possible life together. You'll see."

Ghost

Chapter 17

That morning at three am we kicked shit off in a major way, after Natalia and I got an understanding. We spent a few hours in the Hilton hotel fucking like rabbits in celebration of her being pregnant, and my stepping away from the game in such a way. I'd never seen Natalia freakier. While we were getting things together in our own unique way, Smoke got what was left of our troops rounded up, and ready for action. At three in the morning we were parked in the back of Mikey's big house, with the white picket fence. A house that he'd copped as a duck off from the slums. It was located in a real nice neighborhood on the west side of Memphis.

"Check this out, Phoenix, that's where that bitch nigga lay his head. He fucking with this li'l Asian and Black bitch from Dallas. I think she was a stripper or something, but anyway, she three months pregnant with his shawty. A few of the homies that done had their ear to the streets say he planning on opening up shop in Dallas as well. Shawty got the plug on a whole list of shit because her brothers are in the game real tough up in San Francisco. I hope this nigga in here, but if he ain't, she definitely know where he is, and we gone get that shit out of her. You feel me?"

I tightened the black leather gloves on my hands and wiggled my fingers inside of them. "Less talking, let's go and handle this bidness. I hope he in there, but if he ain't, just remember that shawty ain't that nigga, so, we ain't gotta fuck her over in a major way, especially if she pregnant." I was thinking about the news that Natalia had just given me about her being pregnant. It struck a chord that Mikey's li'l bitch was in the same condition. For some reason, I felt that I needed to show mercy to her because, if I didn't, something bad would happen to Natalia, or our child. I know that was foolish thinking, but it was just how I felt.

"Man, fuck this bitch. I wanna ice this nigga and get the fuck up outta Memphis. The longer we stay in here the more we run the risk of getting caught by these people. Fuck that. Let's roll, big homie."

He slid the Jason Voorhees mask over his face, and tucked both pistols on his waist, opened the door to the truck and stepped out into the night.

I did the same. Loud crickets sounded all around. Lightning bugs floated through the air. It felt like it was over a hundred degrees out. The ski mask on my face began to itch right away. "Bruh, you good?" I asked sensing that something wasn't right with Smoke. He seemed kind of short tempered to me.

"I'm good. Now just ain't the time to be getting all lenient and soft. We got a mission, let's make this shit happen." He hopped the fence in the back yard.

I hopped it and was on his trail. "What the fuck you talking about, bruh?"

He walked twenty more paces in silence, stopped and pointed. "Look, they stupid ass left a window open. Yeah, this gone be sweet." He jogged across the yard.

I followed and caught up to him. I was irritated because he seemed to be ignoring me. The worst lick to pull was a lick with a person who had ill feelings toward you at that time. Anything could have gone wrong. If it did I needed to know that Smoke had my back, not that he would hold back because of some shit he was harboring. I grabbed his arm. "What the fuck wrong wit you, bruh?"

He snatched his arm away. "Get the fuck off of me, Potna. Say Mane, I ain't no nigga's worker. I'm my own man. Plus, I thought we was in this shit together. What, because your cousin get pregnant, now y'all sailing off into the sunset and I'm still supposed to be pounding the pavement? Huh, Mr. King?" He shook his head.

I was at a loss for words. It seemed that he'd heard the entire conversation between me, and Natalia and he was feeling some type of way about it. N'all, it sounded like he was on some jealous shit. That infuriated me. "Nigga, so instead of coming at me like a man, you cop an attitude like a bitch on her period? Get the fuck out of here." I stepped into his face. "Nigga, we finna handle this bidness. Kill Mikey, and then we gon have a nice sit down. Until that time comes, get yo shit together, and focus. Now let's go."

He stood staring at me for a long time. Then nodded. "Yeah, aiight, Phoenix. Let's just handle this shit. We'll talk later." He turned and jogged to the house. Ducked down under the window and looked both ways.

I caught up with him. Scanned the scenery. It appeared quiet. Like the neighborhood was sleeping. That was perfect. All of our guns were silenced by the mechanisms on the end of the barrels, so as long as we prevented any unnecessary screaming we were good to go. I was still feeling some type of way toward Smoke at the moment, but he was a good dude. We'd been through a lot, I was sure we would get past it. We had to.

"Say, Phoenix, give me a boost into their back window. I'ma go in here and see what it do. Then, I'ma open that back door right there for you. I'm letting you know right now, if I see that nigga before I get to the backdoor, I'm wetting his ass up like he grass a something." Smoke stood up and lifted his right Jordan.

I clasped my fingers together and fixed them so he would be able to step into them. He got his foot situated and held my shoulder. Hooped upward and opened the window some more. My dude took a second and looked both ways, before jumping inside of it, and falling to the floor.

I took a pistol out of my waist and cocked it. I waited impatiently for him at the back door for what seemed like an eternity. I was waiting so long that I got spooked that something had happened to him. I was about to jump into the window myself, when the lock on the back door clicked. He pulled it open and waved me inside with a gun in his hand. "What the fuck took you so long, nigga?" I asked feeling my heart pounding in my chest.

"Man, you'll see. That bitch nigga, Mikey, ain't even here. It's three other people that is though. That Asian and Black bitch that I was telling you about, and two niggas that was supposed to be on security for him. At least that's what I think they was supposed to be doing. Here's the kicker, I found all three of they asses in the bed together, fucking. I mean fucking the shit out old girl, too. I got 'em in the living room tied up. Come on. Let's make 'em tell us when that nigga a be coming home."

It took me a few moments to register what Smoke was actually saying. By the time it did, I was inside the house and standing over the naked trio. Smoke had bound their hands with extension cords, and duct taped their mouths. I was impressed by his work. I was unsure if I could have tied up three people all by myself without getting irritated and simply killing at least two of them.

Smoke grabbed the Asian and Black chick by her hair and slammed her again the wall. She screamed into her tape. Her slanted eyes were wide open. She appeared terrified. He grabbed her by the throat. The bump in her flat tummy was barely visible. "Bitch, I'ma ask you this one time and one time only. Where the fuck is Mikey?"

She squeezed her eye lids together. Shook her head. Sweat slid down the side of her forehead. She hollered into the tape as if she was trying to tell him something.

Smoke yanked the tape off of her mouth. "Speak, bitch."

She swallowed. Looked into his eyes and mugged him. "You stupid son of a bitch. Do you have any idea who I am, or what my family is going to do to you when they find out that you've put your hands on me? Do you?" She snapped.

Smoke frowned and pulled a knife out of the sheath in his waistband. He held the long, serrated blade against her cheek. "Bitch, I don't give a fuck who you are, or your punk ass family. I asked you a muthafuckin question, and since you can't answer it like you were supposed to." *Slice!* He whipped the blade across her pretty face, skeeting blood along the wall. It dripped down to her neck and around his gloved hands.

She yelped. Her eyes got as big as saucers. "No, you didn't. No, you didn't. I'm going to kill you, you son of a bitch. You cut my face. You..."

Smoke tightened his hold and sliced her two more times. "Bitch, where is Mikey?" Another slice. "Where is Mikey Bitch?" *Slice.* "You think cause you pregnant that you can ruin my life? *Slice. Slice. Slice.* "That I'ma have sympathy on you? Huh, bitch? Huh? Huh? Huh? Huh? Slice after slice after slice after slice. He hit her so many times with the blade, so fast, that by the time I thought to stop him, she fell in a bloody heap. He stepped away.

She slid onto her back. Her face was mangled. Blood seeped out of her slash wounds and bubbled over to the carpet. It looked horrific. She blinked her eyes and covered her face with her hands.

Smoke grabbed her by the hair again. "Bitch, where is he?"

She began to shake. "Kiss... My.... Ass..." Then her eyes closed.

He dropped her to the floor, kicked her as hard as he could in the stomach. She flipped over and coughed up a glob of blood. "Punk Bitch. How the fuck she gone have this much loyalty for that fuck nigga, but then be in here fucking his mans? Bitches ain't shit. We can't trust these hoes, bruh. We just can't."

I stood there with mixed feelings. Every time I looked down at the pregnant female I saw Natalia's face, and that spooked me. I shouldn't have allowed him to do what he had. I should've stopped that shit before it got that far, but I hadn't. I felt like shit because of it. I shook my head and snatched up one of the naked dudes. Placed my gun to his forehead. "Where the fuck is Mikey? When will he be returning to this mafucka?"

He shook his head. "Mmm. Mmm. Mmm."

I yanked the tape off of his mouth. "Fuck is you saying? Mikey went to Birth Memphis about an hour ago for a drop off. He said he'd be back sometime in the morning or late in the afternoon. Look, Mane, I don't wanna die over his beef. Just let me go. I got three shawties at home. They need their..."

Boof.

His head exploded before he could get his last words out. Blood spattered all across my mask. Pieces of his meat went inside of my eye holes. It was hot and squishy. His body slumped the ground, bleeding profusely.

I jumped back in shock. Stunned. "What the fuck, bruh?"

Smoke stood holding the smoking gun. "I always hated them simp type niggas. How the fuck that fine bitch have more heart than him? That don't make no sense whatsoever. Do it?" He aimed his gun down at the last surviving victim. "Say, bitch nigga, I'ma let you live so you can tell this tale. Tell that fuck nigga, Mikey, that his ass is grass. That when the Duffle Bag Cartel catch his ass, we gon blow his bitch ass off of the map. You hear me?"

The dude nodded his head furiously, groaning into his duct tape. His scary ass flopped on the floor to further emphasize his point.

I stood over him and blazed him with six shots, all facials. Those shots knocked hefty chunks out of his mug. The sparks from my gun lit up the living room again and again. Once I confirmed that he was no longer breathing, I turned to Smoke. "Nigga, ain't no way we about to leave this bitch nigga alive so he can tell the authorities everythang that happened. We'll find Mikey. Memphis is small. Let's get the fuck up out of here. These mafuckas starting to stink." I stepped over the last body.

Smoke stepped into my path. "Say, Mane, I wanted his bitch ass to stay alive so we could send Mikey's bitch ass into a frenzy. If Mikey would of came home to find dude's pussy ass stretched out in a puddle of blood he would been more susceptible to run around like a chicken wit his head cut off. It would have been easier to smoke his pussy ass. You dig me? You aint king of their shit just yet." He clenched his teeth.

I moved nose to nose wit him. "That nigga dead. I made that call. That's what it is. You can quit all this tough shit and fall yo ass in line. Move, nigga." I bumped his ass out of the way and headed toward the back door. Once there, I jogged down the steps and broke out of the backyard, and down the alley. I had the engine to the truck already started by the time Smoke appeared.

He jumped inside of the truck and slammed the door. "Say, Phoenix, we gon need to get an understanding. I don't like you going behind me and doing whatever the fuck you think is kosher. I been grinding in Memphis ever since I was eight years old. I know how to fuck these slums, Potna."

He was starting to get me heated. I could only hold my temper for so long before I lost my mind on a nigga's ass. Smoke was my li'l homie. I didn't like feeling the way that I was currently feeling about him. "Smoke, what you got in your chest, homie? You feel like you need to knuckle up a something?"

He pulled his nose. "I ain't ducking no action that's fa damn show."

I nodded. "Awright then, nigga. We gon handle this bidness like Orange Mound niggas. Den once that shit over we gon get an understanding. Cool?"

"Cool, nigga."

Chapter 18

I took my shirt off, and handed it to Natalia, just as the rain began to fall from the sky. Lightning flashed, illuminating the roof of the project building we were on top of. From this vantage point we could over look the entire Orange Mound. This was our home, and in our home when two men had a dispute they settled it with their knuckles and moved on from the situation. I felt like Smoke needed his ass whooped. I was the big homie. It was my place to put his ass in line.

Natalia stepped in front of me. The rain had caused her long, curly hair to mat to her head. The water dripped off of her curls and made her look fine as could be. "Daddy, this isn't smart. There is nothing you can gain from whooping your li'l guy. If you whoop him, he's going to feel resentment in his heart for you. You'll have to watch him and your back for as long as you deal with him. That's ridiculous. On the other hand, if he whoops you you're going to want to kill him. Especially if he does it in front of me. I know how you are. So, please don't do this." Her blue eyes sparkled in the night.

Our hittas from our Cartel came onto the roof and formed a big circle. They stood side by side with masks on their faces. Smoke stepped into the circle and removed his shirt. He bounced up and down and rolled his head around on his neck. "Let's handle this bidness, Phoenix. We got the whole family watching now. Hopefully at the end of all this you'll honor my gansta." He continued to bounce up and down.

I got ready to step into the circle. Natalia pulled my arm. "Baby, this is dumb. I got a gut feeling telling me so.

Please, don't do this. I am begging you." She wiped rain water from the side of my face.

"Fuck taking so long Phoenix? Let's get the show on the road, baby."

I nudged Natalia aside, and stepped into the circle. The rain began to fall harder from the sky. It pitter pattered on the cement of the rooftop. My heart was beating hard in my chest. It had been a while since I'd knuckled up with any nigga. I didn't know what my hand game was going to be like after so long. In addition to that, I'd never boxed a nigga I was cool with. I didn't know how far to take things, or if I would be able to let them go if he handed me a loss.

He stepped into my face. "I ain't nobody's slave, Phoenix. You ain't gon pimp the fuck out of my hustle and reap all of the benefits while you stay in some fucking suburb and think you gon be calling the shots. Nall, Potna, you gon respect me as an equal. That bitch supposed to be working for the both of us. Cousin or no cousin. Period." He pushed me as hard as he could, and swung, hitting me in the jaw. "Let's get it."

I stumbled back and regained my balance on the slippery pavement. Although I was stunned, I gathered myself, and rushed him, swinging haymakers. The first one caught him under the cheek bone. The second one missed.

He jumped back, and lunged forward, swinging fast, and hard. "Fuck, nigga."

I slapped two punches away before I threw up my guards, ducked and came back with an uppercut. It caught him on the chin.

Smoke staggered backwards and fell on his ass. He sat there for a minute and shook his head. The rain splashed off of his body. It dripped down his face. Lightning flashed across the sky. It gave me a chance to see Natalia's worried face. The crowd urged Smoke to get up.

I paced back and forth in the circle. Had it been anybody else, that Orange Mound shit in me would have caused me to stomp him out within an inch of his life. But, this was my li'l nigga, so I waited for him to get up.

He came to his feet and popped his neck on both sides. Smoke shook his arms out, jumping up and down. "Aiight. Good shit. I ain't gon fall for that no more though." He approached me with his guards protecting his face.

"You ready, li'l nigga?" I asked, refusing to wait for him to respond. Instead, I gave him a hard jab, and broke through his guards with a left hook. That sent him flying backward.

He caught his balance, ducked all the way down, and punched me in the nuts so hard that I couldn't help falling to my knees and throwing up a little. Smoke took that opening to kick me in the chest. I fell on the ground. He jumped on top of me, swinging blow after blow into my face. Fucking me up. Them punches hurt so bad that I heard myself making some weird ass noises. Every punch that he made contact with felt like I was being hit by some giant ass monkey knuckles. He busted my lip, my eye and swole up my cheek.

I brought my knee upward into his groin with all of my might. I felt his family jewels crunch. He hollered out and fell off of me. I staggered. Blood ran from my mouth. My nuts felt like they'd been smashed individually by a sledge hammer.

Smoke crawled around on the ground. "I'm finna fuck you up, Phoenix. I'm tired of this shit. I ain't finna play these games wit you." He swore, coming to his feet.

Natalia ran into the circle. "Y'all are like brothers. Stop this shit. It's stupid. We need to focus on Mikey. Not each other." She hollered.

"Get her out of the battle field. Take her ass over there. Now! That's an order!" Smoke snapped.

Two of our Cartel members got ready to manhandle Natalia. She stepped back in fear and pulled a Forty Five from her purse. "One of you muthafuckas touch me and I swear to God, somebody gon die. Now test me. Get the fuck back!"

The two dudes moved backward with their hands shoulder length high. Thunder roared in the sky. Lightning flashed again. The wind picked up speed. It became violent in nearly an instant.

"Y'all, get away from my baby, Mane. That's my Queen right there." The wind began to blow so hard that I started to freeze. I wanted this fight to be over with. Looking off into the distance, it looked like a funnel cloud was forming. "Smoke, this shit over with, li'l Homie. You got that shit out if your system yet?"

He wiped the blood from his nose. "Hell n'all, nigga. We gon finish this shit once and for all." He struggled to maintain his balance, but the wind made it hard for that to happen.

"Guys! It says on my weather app that there is a tornado forming and it's going to be coming through this county. We need to get the fuck out of here."

"No! Me and Phoenix gon finish this shit! All you want him to do is be all up yo ass anyway. For God sakes, he's your cousin. Now you walking around pregnant by him."

I rushed toward him. "Hey! Leave her out of this, nigga. What the fuck is wrong with you?"

He met me half way, swinging like a maniac. "Fuck both of y'all. Y'all don't give a fuck about me." He hit me with eight hard punches. Three of them broke through and landed against my face. The wind blew harder and towed us about.

I fell to the ground and bounced right back up. Scooped him and dumped him on his back. "Get yo tough ass up, nigga. Come on." I was no longer going to take it easy on him. Just like he was trying to give me the bidness,

I was going to give him some as well, with no mercy. "Get the fuck up." A hard kick to the ribs sent him on his back.

Natalia rushed and pulled me away. "Baby, come on. Look, the Tornado is right over there." She pointed.

No more than five blocks away was a fully formed tornado. It busted through an apartment building and kept going, headed in our direction. This was the third tornado that we'd gotten in the year of twenty nineteen.

I took her hand and rushed over to Smoke. "Come on, bruh. Let's get the fuck out of here."

He jumped up and pushed me. "Fuck you, Phoenix. I thought you was by nigga, man. You know I ain't got no fucking family. Only my kids man. Now you trying to run off with Natalia and leave a nigga in the lurch. That's foul, Playboy. Foul as a muthafucka."

The harsh winds blew and knocked all of us down. I felt as if I was being pulled across the roof. I could hear members of the Cartel screaming for dear life. The rain felt like a broken geyser. I was wishing that I had any kind of shirt on to cover my bare flesh. I was so cold that I was shivering. It felt like I was being tortured.

I pulled Natalia to her feet. Then the both of us helped Smoke get to his. Everybody ran for the door of the roof.

We were like a group of people trying to rush into one elevator. The roof began to shake. I felt like I was being vacuumed. A loud whistling of the wind made its presence known.

"Phoenix! Daddy! It's pulling me!" Natalia screamed. Her long hair waved like a flag behind her.

I wrapped my arms around her. It seemed as if somebody was trying to pull her from my grasps. Ahead of us the doorway was congested by bodies trying to rush into it. They fell over each other as the tornado got so close that I could smell the difference in the atmosphere. The loud whirring spooked the shit out of me. We had to get into this door.

Smoke pushed the last few members into the door and pulled Natalia's wrist to help her get inside. I fell right along with her. The tornado caused the metal door to slam so hard that it folded inward. Then it was sucked away altogether. It flew into the air, as the wind attacked the hallway. Pulling us upward.

"Grab the banister. Grab the banister! Hurry!" Natalia advised.

I grabbed the banister just before two dudes went flying past me, up the stairs, and out of the open door. They hollered the whole time, before disappearing into the whirring wind. I continued to hold on as best I could, but it was so hard to do.

"Phoenix! My shit slipping Bruh. I'm slipping. Aw shit! I'm slipping." The wind blew and appeared to pick up strength.

Just as his fingers slipped off of the banister I caught his hand. Took a hold of his wrist and held on to him. "Hold on Mikey. Hold on, Bruh." I started saying all kinds of prayers in my head. Begging Jehovah to save us from this natural disaster. This plague that He'd sent down on us. The tornado seemed to hover for ten seconds or longer, then it went on its way. As soon as it left the area of the roof door we fell on the steps hard. Groaning in pain. I rushed to Natalia's side. "Baby? Are you okay? You didn't hurt your stomach did you?"

She winced in pain. "I don't know. I don't think so." She wrapped her arm around it and took a few deep breaths.

"You saved my life Phoenix. Muthafucka, you saved my life. Damn, dawg. I can't believe this shit. I don't know if I could have done the same thing for you, Mane. Fuck, I would have been dead." He spit a glob of blood on to the stair well.

**

Natalia climbed over my body and rested her head on my chest. We were fresh out of the shower and laid up in a penthouse suite inside of the Hilton Hotel. She'd been shaking ever since we'd came back from the traumatic event with the tornado. "Baby, I thought I was about to lose you. First up there on that roof, and secondly when the Tornado hit. I don't know what I would do without you. I just love you so much." She rubbed over my chest and kissed me right above my heart.

"I thought I was about to lose you too Boo. But we got through that shit. That's all that matters. "Get up here." I pulled her atop my body.

She straddled me, rested her small, soft hands on my chest and looked into my eyes. "Phoenix. Can you be honest with me about something?" Her ice blue eyes seemed to pierce my soul.

I gripped that fat ass booty that was encased in a pair of red lace boy shorts. "Of course, baby. What's on your mind?" I continued to rub all over her backside. It felt so soft and warm. I could never get enough of the feel of it.

"Daddy, do you think there will ever be a time when you can look at me as a woman and no longer your family? I guess I'm just wondering if we'll ever be able to take things to the next level?"

Man, I loved Natalia. I didn't give a fuck about that cousin shit no more. I was crazy about Natalia. I dug her physically, loved how she was set up mentally, and emotionally. Besides Kamya, I don't think there was any female that I'd ever come close to loving as much as I did her. There was something about her that drove me crazy. "Baby, I don't care about that cousin relationship. I love you. I wanna be with you, and I am glad that you're having our child. I don't even think I give a fuck about crushing Mikey no more. I just want to fly off and be happy with you and Shantê. Alicia is a whole other story. I still don't know what I'ma do about her."

Natalia exhaled slowly. "I forgot all about her. Dang. Didn't she have a li'l boy? Your li'l boy?"

"Yeah, I mean I'm pretty sure it's mine."

Natalia turned her back to me. "So, what are you saying? You don't know for sure?"

"N'all I don't, but by the looks of the child, and giving her the benefit of the doubt. Man, I'm sho he's my seed."

"Well, I mean maybe we should get in touch with her before we leave Memphis, that way you can figure out what you're going to do. Do you have any hidden feelings for her or anything? I need to know before I continue to fall so deeply for you."

I stepped behind her and pulled her to my chest. "The only woman I love and care about in this world is you Natalia. You're my baby. I mean that shit."

She turned around and slid her arms onto my shoulders, stepped on her tippy toes, and kissed me. "Well, you do what you need to do with her so we can get out of here. Time is ticking."

Ghost

Chapter 19

Alicia stepped into the diner, pushing a stroller with a hood pulled over her head. She stopped and scanned the small roadside restaurant, spotted me in the far back corner, and made her way in my direction.

There were men from my Cartel stationed at five different tables, and two rolling around the parking lot on the look out for the authorities or anything out of the blue. I felt real uneasy being back in Memphis. I just wanted to get an understanding with Alicia and get a move on. The situation with Mikey was still nagging at me, but I was doing the best that I could to focus on other things that were more important. At least for the moment. When Alicia got close to where I was sitting, I stood up.

She pushed the stroller as close to the table as possible before she pulled back the covering so I could see our son's face. She had him bundled up as if it was freezing cold outside. His li'l caramel face was pudgy. His brows thick as mine. His eye lids were closed. He looked so much like Shanté it was uncanny. "Hey, Phoenix. Why did you want to see me? You said it was urgent."

I took her hand and helped her to take a seat. She sat across from me, and peered down at our son twice before she finally settled in. I could tell that Alicia was going to be one of those overprotective mothers. "Alicia the reason I called you out here is because I'm about to leave, shawty. I'm talking about for a long time. I'm sure you already know that the police are looking for me for a whole bunch of stuff that I won't get into ."

"You don't need to get into it Phoenix. It's all online. They got you as the suspect for so many crimes that it's amazing that you're still walking around right now. The only reason I came is because I didn't know if it was going to be my last time seeing you. if it is, I wanted you to see your son one final time." Alicia peered down at him. She looked sad.

I shook by head and lowered it. "Damn."

"What?"

"Alicia, I'm sorry that things turned out this way. I guess I should have never been pursuing you behind the homie's back like I was. I should have allowed for you to live a happy life. I've just always been so attracted and addicted to you. for obvious reasons. I know that ain't an excuse, but it's the truth."

"Yeah well, you're right. You should have left me alone. Especially of you didn't have a game plan to make sure that the consequences of your actions were going to make sense for more than just you. You've always been extremely selfish Phoenix. Ruining peoples lives, and only staying inside of them for as long as they make sense to you. It's not right, and it's no way to live. I will never forgive you for what you did to me. For what you did to us." She laid her hand on Phoenix Jr.'s chest., then glared at me with anger. "Despite how you did me, I still love you, and I wish you the best. That's me being honest."

I took the duffle bag from beside me and slid it across the table. "Huh, it's five hundred thousand in cash in this bag. It's yours. I know it ain't much, but it'll be a start. I'ma still do my part for you, and for Jr. Right now, I just gotta get my shit together. Once I tie up these loose ends then I'll send for you and him. Cool?"

Alicia took the bag and unzipped it. She looked inside and trailed her hand through all of the cash inside. Scoffed, and slammed the bag on the side of her booth. "Money. That's what it's always been about for you, Phoenix. You think that money can solve everything. Don't you understand that we have a whole ass son that needs a father. Somebody to mold him into being a man. That money can only provide for his necessities on the outside, but what's most important for him will need to come from you. You need to mold him internally. I can't be his mother and father. It's your job to be his dad. I just don't know what to think right now. Where are you running off to?"

"I'm not running off nowhere. I'm creating some distance between myself and Tennessee for a little while. It's real hot here, and it's only smart that I create some distance. So that's what I'ma do."

"Okay so why we ain't going with you?"

That caught me off guard. "What?"

"You heard me. Clearly if you can throw a bag of money at me in this amount, then you can provide for me and your son to come with you wherever you are going. Do you know that Mikey has out a decree that whoever finds me, and cuts myself and Phoenix Jr's head off he'll give them two Trap houses one for each head, and product at half price? Huh? Did you know that?"

I felt sick. "That bitch ass nigga. N'all, I ain't know that. Why would he do something like that?" I asked stupidly.

She stared at me as if I'd lost my mind. "Are you really asking me that right now?"

I shook my head. "N'all, forget it. You serious? You wanna come with me?" Alicia had always been so independent. I couldn't imagine her following up behind me, but she really must've been worried. I knew how shit was in Memphis when it came to a come up. Mafuckas would do anything to come up on a morsel, so with Mikey offering two trap houses and product at half price, it was only a matter if time before somebody cashed in on that offer. If I got wherever I was going and found out that my son, and Alicia's head had been cut off I would never forgive myself.

"Where else am I going to go Phoenix? I ain't got no family here no more. All of my people done moved back west, and we're barely in speaking terms. I dropped a lot of them for Mikey. So, my only option for myself and for our son is to come wherever you're going. Wait a minute, unless you're going with a female of some sort. Is that the case?" She looked into my eyes.

I diverted my gaze. "Yeah, that's the case, but it won't stop me from doing what I need to do for you and him."

She stood up. "You've lost your fucking mind. You think I'm going to come a long for the ride while you have me and some other female. Boy bye." She grabbed the bag of money and took the stoppers off of the stroller wheels. "I'll see you in another life Phoenix. I wish you all the best, I really do."

I stood up and grabbed her wrist. "Hold yo li'l ass on Alicia, damn. Bae, we ain't decided nothing. You need to hear me out. If you ain't trying to come with me, then where are you going? We need to stay in touch so I can do my part no matter where I am."

She snatched her wrist away from me. "Don't worry about it. I'll find my way. I don't need you or any other man. Me and my child will be fine. Trust and believe that. I am a woman. The strongest being on earth." She attempted to leave again.

I blocked her path. "Alicia, let me at least foot the bill. I'll pay for you to live anywhere on earth. I'll make sure that you never have to worry about any bills ever again.

Whatever you want I'll make sure that you get it. You gotta at least let me do that."

She looked up at me and turned up her nose. "You really don't get it, do you? Do you honestly think that I risked all of that stuff with Mikey because I wanted you to provide for me? Are you serious right now, Phoenix? I'm not incompetent. I don't need no man to provide for me. Whatever we need, I will take care of it. You can take your propositions, and your selfish ways, and go on with your life. We don't need you Phoenix. I will always love you, but I will never respect you for what you've done to me. Please have a nice life." She pushed the stroller around me and left the diner. As much as I wanted to pursue her, I knew that Alicia was stubborn. It would have been a lost cause.

***

That night I felt sick to my stomach. I was really regretting not chasing behind her. After all, she had my son. I should have made more of an effort. I couldn't help fixating on everything she'd said about me. I wondered if, deep down, they were all true. I honestly felt like shit.

Natalia, sauntered into the hotel room, and sat down on the bed next to me. "Daddy, I can tell that something ain't right. Do you want to talk about it?" She took my hand and rubbed the back of it.

"I went and hollered at Alicia today. I asked her if there was anything that I could do for her and my son, but she shot me down real hard. Told me what she really think about me and wasn't none of it good. I knew her for a long time, and I always thought the world of her. To hear her talk like she did, to say what she really thought about me was enough to crush my soul, that's all."

Natalia continued to rub the back of my hand. "Well, baby, how about I tell you what I really think about you. I think that you are the most handsome man in all of his world. I think that you are going to be an incredible father to our child, just as you are to Shanté. I love you with all of my heart, and I don't wanna be with anybody other than you, Phoenix. I know that you've been through a lot. You've hurt many people, and vice versa, but I accept you as you are. You belong to me, and that's all that matters. When it comes to Alicia, don't worry. We'll track her for the rest if her life and just deposit large sums of cash into her bank account two or three times a month. She'll never have to be in need of anything. We'll make sure of that. Okay, daddy?"

Damn, Natalia always had a way of making me feel better. She was my rock. The longer we stayed together the further I fell in love with her. All of those things were exactly what I needed to hear. She made me feel so much stronger. "Thank you for saying what you said baby. I love you to death. I need you, do you know that?" I pulled her up so she could sit on my lap.

She laid her head on my shoulder. "Baby, I need you too. You're my daddy. You make me feel so complete, and from here on out it's us against the world. Ain't nothing or no one gon change that. I mean it." She kissed my neck, then rested her face right in the crux of it. "You're a phenomenal man, Phoenix. Once a woman gets the chance to understand you, only then can she love you in the way that I do. We are two of the same kind."

I kissed her forehead and held her tighter, then I slipped my hand under her white beater, and rubbed her soft tummy. "Things are going to be different with this one. I'ma make sure that this baby has everything that it needs.

That you and I remain together, and strong. I just want us to be strong and happy, baby. You're the best thing to ever happen to me." I ran my fingers through her hair and turned her face to mine. I kissed her soft, juicy lips, sucked them into my mouth, and licked all over them. She tasted like mint. Her breathing increased, along with my own. Suddenly she was straddling me. The beater moved up her hips and exposed the bottom portion of her ass cheeks. I fell back on the bed.

She leaned down and rubbed her nose back and forth across my own. "I love you, Phoenix. I don't care what this world thinks. I freaking love you, and I'ma hold you down for the rest of my life. Not only are we going to conquer the United States, but we're going to conquer this entire world, if that's what you wanna do. I live to make you happy, baby. Just you." She kissed my lips again.

My hands palmed her ass. Our tongues played all over each other's. Lips sucked loudly. My fingers slipped into the leg holes of her panties. I rubbed her pussy lips. They had a hint of stubble on them. Her crease was already leaking it's juices. My middle finger slipped inside of her. I pulled it out and sucked the juices off. She tasted so sweet and forbidden. "Where we gon go, baby?"

"Wherever you wanna go, Phoenix. I say we do a bunch of traveling, and wherever we wind up, we wind up. What do you say?"

That sounded good to me. Her jet could take us any where we wanted to go. The only thing that we had to remain conscious of was the fact that both of us were wanted. Me by the feds, and the state of Tennessee and her by the Russians. I was a Memphis nigga. I didn't really have a clue what took place outside of the city, so when it came to all of that traveling and geographical shit, she would have to lead the way until I was able to master the world outside of the slums of Memphis. Before I could let her know what I was thinking, there was a loud knock on the door.

I tossed Natalia onto the bed, stood up and rushed to the pillow and grabbed my gun from under it. She did the same. Then I was standing on the side of the door. "Who is it?"

"It's Smoke, nigga, open the door."

I slowly stepped over to the peephole and looked out . Smoke stood in front of it with sweat peppered along his forehead. His top lip was still busted from when I'd had to touch him up a li'l bit. I opened the door.

He rushed in but topped when he saw Natalia in her state of undress and looked her up and down hungrily. "Damn."

"Nigga, focus. What the fuck going on?"

Natalia eased into the bathroom and closed the door, after picking her clothes up from the floor. "Beating like he was the damn police. Jesus Christ, Smoke." She chastised.

He shook his head. "That's my bad, bruh, but what I'm finna tell you is going to blow your mind."

Chapter 20

I made another revolution around Toya and shook my head. "So, dis what that betrayal shit look like, huh?" I asked.

She struggled against her bonds and frowned her face and looked up to me. "You know what, fuck you, Phoenix. You think you all that. I swear to God, one day you're going to get everything you deserve. I hope I'm the one behind the trigger, too. Bitch ass nigga."

I knelt in front of her face. "What did I do to you, Shawty?"

She scoffed and tried to yank one of her hands free. Smoke had tied them to the arms of the chair by the using duct tape. He'd done the same with her ankles. "Nigga, you killed the only man that gave a fuck about me, and for what? All because you was on some jealous shit. And nigga you don't even wanna be with me. That's what makes shit even worse. I swear, I hate you so much that every time I hear your name it feels like my ears are bleeding. I hope Mikey catches you and cut you up into little bitty pieces. It's crazy how you snaked him for his broad. Typical, selfish ass ,Phoenix." She spit on the warehouse floor. "Dis who y'all following behind? Huh? Smoke I promise you this nigga gon stab you in your back as soon as he get the chance . You gotta be the dumbest nigga in the world to be loyal to him after you've seen how he get down. Everybody that he's ever been close to, he fucked them over in one way or the other. Common sense should tell yo stupid ass to dump his ass and do your own thing. But, you'll learn. Ain't that right, Phoenix?"

Smoke stepped into her face and slapped her so hard that she fell on her side along with the chair. "Bruh, you letting this bitch use a lot of her word count. If you want,

I'll snuff her ass. A bitch that talk that much need to lose her life."

Toya laughed. Her mouth was filled with blood. "You bitch ass nigga. Didn't he just beat the fuck out of you on some roof in Orange Mound? Now, you're sucking his dick like one of those project hoes. You're funnier than Kevin Hart." She busted up laughing and swallowed the blood that was in her mouth. "I ain't scared of either one of you niggas. Do what the fuck you gon do. Ain't nothing in this life but heartache and pain anyway."

Smoke grabbed her up by her micro braids. "Punk bitch, you gon keep running your mouth right?" He pulled out an Army knife with a serrated blade. Held it to her throat. "Let me off this bitch, Phoenix. I just got wind that she bodied a few of the homies from out of the Mound. She been rolling with them Black Haven niggas real tough anyway. She the enemy." He pressed the blade to her throat and began to slowly slice across it. A trickle of blood appeared.

"Wait!" I rushed over to him and pulled his hand back.

He jumped up. "What the fuck, nigga?" He had a mean scowl on his face.

"Nigga, this still my baby's mother. If any mafucka gon take her out the game it's gon be me." I pulled her up and slammed her in the chair so hard she yelped in pain.

Smoke stepped back and sucked his gold teeth. "Yeah, aiight, Phoenix. Handle yo bidness then."

Toya laughed. "Phoenix ain't bout that life. He ain't gon do shit to me. I most definitely ain't worried. I'm his daughter's mother. Ain't that right, baby?"

Smack.

I slapped her across thee face so hard, that she spit blood across the room. "Shut the fuck up. Shawty this ain't that. Far as I'm concerned you deserted my daughter a long time ago, and love don't live here anymore. Now, what's good wit Mikey? Where that bitch nigga at, and how long y'all been fucking around?" I was glad I didn't have my pistol on me. I didn't know if I would have used it on her ass or not, but she had me heated.

Blood ran off of her chin. "Mikey more of a man than you'll ever be. When he get a hold of you, he gon shred yo punk ass. He just put two million dollars on yo head. If you think you're about to make it out of Memphis, you're out of your rabbit ass mind. He already got your bitch."

A chill went down my spine. "My bitch? Who da the fuck you talking bout?"

She laughed. "Poor, slow ass, Phoenix. You're always the last one to find out about things. You ain't heard what happened to Alicia this afternoon?"

"Ain't nothing happened to her. I just saw shawty and she was good."

Toya shook her head, and a trail of blood slid in to her bottom lip and dripped off of her chin. "N'all you saw her first, but it's what happened to her after she left you that's what's really good. All I can say is that there is more to her to love. About a hundred pieces more. Ain't no more Junior either. Life is a bitch, ain't it?" She busted up laughing.

I didn't know whether to believe her or if she was pulling the wool over my eyes. "Bitch, you lying. I just seen her."

Smoke shook his head. "Nall, bruh. She ain't."

I looked up to him and frowned. "What the fuck you mean she ain't? How would you know?"

Smoke took two pistols from behind his back and aimed them at me. He cocked the hammers and curled his lip. "Cut I cut that bitch up at Mikey's request, and that ain't all. "Yo Mikey, come on out big Homie. Let's quit playing games with this nigga."

I took two steps back as Mikey appeared with a bound Natalia. He threw her at my feet and kicked her as hard as he could in her back. She screamed in pain. Her eyes were both blackened. He held a Forty Glock in his right hand. "Yo bitch got a five million dollar bounty on her head. Whew. That was too much money to pass up even for Smoke. They say revenge is a dish best served cold, Phoenix. I'ma bout to test that theory. Smoke tie this nigga up, we about to have some fun. After his tortuous death, I am officially announcing my leadership of the Duffle Bag Cartel."

To Be Continued...
Duffle Bag Cartel 4
Coming Soon

Submission Guideline

Submit the first three chapters of your completed manuscript to ldpsubmissions@gmail.com, subject line: Your book's title. The manuscript must be in a .doc file and sent as an attachment. Document should be in Times New Roman, double spaced and in size 12 font. Also, provide your synopsis and full contact information. If sending multiple submissions, they must each be in a separate email.

Have a story but no way to send it electronically? You can still submit to LDP/Ca$h Presents. Send in the first three chapters, written or typed, of your completed manuscript to:

LDP: Submissions Dept
Po Box 870494
Mesquite, Tx 75187

DO NOT send original manuscript. Must be a duplicate.

Provide your synopsis and a cover letter containing your full contact information.

Thanks for considering LDP and Ca$h Presents.

<u>Coming Soon from Lock Down Publications/Ca$h Presents</u>

BOW DOWN TO MY GANGSTA

By **Ca$h**

TORN BETWEEN TWO

By **Coffee**

BLOOD STAINS OF A SHOTTA **III**

By **Jamaica**

STEADY MOBBIN **III**

By **Marcellus Allen**

BLOOD OF A BOSS **VI**

By **Askari**

LOYAL TO THE GAME **IV**

LIFE OF SIN **III**

By **T.J. & Jelissa**

A DOPEBOY'S PRAYER **II**

By **Eddie "Wolf" Lee**

IF LOVING YOU IS WRONG... **III**

LOVE ME EVEN WHEN IT HURTS **III**

By **Jelissa**

TRUE SAVAGE **VII**

By **Chris Green**

BLAST FOR ME **III**

DUFFLE BAG CARTEL **IV**

By **Ghost**

ADDICTIED TO THE DRAMA **III**

By **Jamila Mathis**

A HUSTLER'S DECEIT 3

KILL ZONE **II**

BAE BELONGS TO ME III

SOUL OF A MONSTER

By **Aryanna**

THE COST OF LOYALTY **III**

By **Kweli**

SHE FELL IN LOVE WITH A REAL ONE **II**

By **Tamara Butler**

RENEGADE BOYS **III**

By **Meesha**

CORRUPTED BY A GANGSTA **IV**

By **Destiny Skai**

A GANGSTER'S SYN II

By **J-Blunt**

KING OF NEW YORK V

RISE TO POWER III

COKE KINGS II

By **T.J. Edwards**

GORILLAZ IN THE BAY III

De'Kari

THE STREETS ARE CALLING II

Duquie Wilson

KINGPIN KILLAZ IV

STREET KINGS 2

PAID IN BLOOD 2

Hood Rich

SINS OF A HUSTLA II

ASAD

TRIGGADALE II

Elijah R. Freeman

MARRIED TO A BOSS III

By Destiny Skai & Chris Green

KINGS OF THE GAME III

Playa Ray

SLAUGHTER GANG II

By Willie Slaughter

Available Now

RESTRAINING ORDER **I & II**

By **CA$H & Coffee**

LOVE KNOWS NO BOUNDARIES **I II & III**

By **Coffee**

RAISED AS A GOON I, II, III & IV

BRED BY THE SLUMS I, II, III

BLAST FOR ME I & II

ROTTEN TO THE CORE I III

A BRONX TALE I, II, III

DUFFEL BAG CARTEL I II III

By **Ghost**

LAY IT DOWN **I & II**

LAST OF A DYING BREED

BLOOD STAINS OF A SHOTTA I & II

By **Jamaica**

LOYAL TO THE GAME

LOYAL TO THE GAME II

LOYAL TO THE GAME III

LIFE OF SIN I, II

By **TJ & Jelissa**

BLOODY COMMAS I & II

SKI MASK CARTEL I II & III

KING OF NEW YORK I II,III IV

RISE TO POWER I II

COKE KINGS

By **T.J. Edwards**

IF LOVING HIM IS WRONG…I & II

LOVE ME EVEN WHEN IT HURTS I II

By **Jelissa**

WHEN THE STREETS CLAP BACK I & II III

By **Jibril Williams**

A DISTINGUISHED THUG STOLE MY HEART I II & III

LOVE SHOULDN'T HURT I II III IV

RENEGADE BOYS I & II

By **Meesha**

A GANGSTER'S CODE I &, II III

A GANGSTER'S SYN

By **J-Blunt**

PUSH IT TO THE LIMIT

By **Bre' Hayes**

BLOOD OF A BOSS **I, II, III, IV, V**

Ghost

By **Askari**

THE STREETS BLEED MURDER **I, II & III**

THE HEART OF A GANGSTA I II& III

By **Jerry Jackson**

CUM FOR ME

CUM FOR ME 2

CUM FOR ME 3

CUM FOR ME 4

An **LDP Erotica Collaboration**

BRIDE OF A HUSTLA **I II & II**

THE FETTI GIRLS **I, II& III**

CORRUPTED BY A GANGSTA I, II & III

By **Destiny Skai**

WHEN A GOOD GIRL GOES BAD

By **Adrienne**

THE COST OF LOYALTY

By Kweli

A GANGSTER'S REVENGE **I II III & IV**

THE BOSS MAN'S DAUGHTERS

THE BOSS MAN'S DAUGHTERS II

THE BOSSMAN'S DAUGHTERS III

THE BOSSMAN'S DAUGHTERS IV

THE BOSS MAN'S DAUGHTERS **V**

A SAVAGE LOVE **I & II**

BAE BELONGS TO ME I II

A HUSTLER'S DECEIT I, II, III

WHAT BAD BITCHES DO I, II, III

180

By **Aryanna**

A KINGPIN'S AMBITON

A KINGPIN'S AMBITION **II**

I MURDER FOR THE DOUGH

By **Ambitious**

TRUE SAVAGE

TRUE SAVAGE II

TRUE SAVAGE **III**

TRUE SAVAGE **IV**

TRUE SAVAGE **V**

TRUE SAVAGE **VI**

By **Chris Green**

A DOPEBOY'S PRAYER

By **Eddie "Wolf" Lee**

THE KING CARTEL **I, II & III**

By **Frank Gresham**

THESE NIGGAS AIN'T LOYAL **I, II & III**

By **Nikki Tee**

GANGSTA SHYT **I II &III**

By **CATO**

THE ULTIMATE BETRAYAL

By **Phoenix**

BOSS'N UP **I , II & III**

By **Royal Nicole**

I LOVE YOU TO DEATH

By **Destiny J**

I RIDE FOR MY HITTA

I STILL RIDE FOR MY HITTA

By **Misty Holt**

LOVE & CHASIN' PAPER

By **Qay Crockett**

TO DIE IN VAIN

SINS OF A HUSTLA

By **ASAD**

BROOKLYN HUSTLAZ

By **Boogsy Morina**

BROOKLYN ON LOCK I & II

By **Sonovia**

GANGSTA CITY

By **Teddy Duke**

A DRUG KING AND HIS DIAMOND I & II III

A DOPEMAN'S RICHES

HER MAN, MINE'S TOO I, II

CASH MONEY HO'S

By Nicole Goosby

TRAPHOUSE KING **I II & III**

KINGPIN KILLAZ I II III

STREET KINGS

PAID IN BLOOD

By **Hood Rich**

LIPSTICK KILLAH **I, II, III**

CRIME OF PASSION I & II

By **Mimi**

STEADY MOBBN' **I, II, III**

By **Marcellus Allen**

WHO SHOT YA **I, II, III**

Renta

GORILLAZ IN THE BAY **I II**

DE'KARI

TRIGGADALE

Elijah R. Freeman

GOD BLESS THE TRAPPERS I, II, III

THESE SCANDALOUS STREETS I, II, III

FEAR MY GANGSTA I, II, III

THESE STREETS DON'T LOVE NOBODY I, II

BURY ME A G I, II, III, IV, V

A GANGSTA'S EMPIRE I, II, III

Tranay Adams

THE STREETS ARE CALLING

Duquie Wilson

MARRIED TO A BOSS... I II

By Destiny Skai & Chris Green

KINGS OF THE GAME I II

Playa Ray

SLAUGHTER GANG II

By Willie Slaughter

BOOKS BY LDP'S CEO, CA$H

<u>TRUST IN NO MAN</u>

<u>TRUST IN NO MAN 2</u>

<u>TRUST IN NO MAN 3</u>

<u>BONDED BY BLOOD</u>

<u>SHORTY GOT A THUG</u>

<u>THUGS CRY</u>

<u>THUGS CRY 2</u>

<u>THUGS CRY 3</u>

<u>TRUST NO BITCH</u>

<u>TRUST NO BITCH 2</u>

<u>TRUST NO BITCH 3</u>

<u>TIL MY CASKET DROPS</u>

<u>RESTRAINING ORDER</u>

<u>RESTRAINING ORDER 2</u>

<u>IN LOVE WITH A CONVICT</u>

<u>Coming Soon</u>

BONDED BY BLOOD 2

BOW DOWN TO MY GANGSTA

Duffle Bag Cartel 3

CPSIA information can be obtained
at www.ICGtesting.com
Printed in the USA
LVHW081544260520
656397LV00009B/371